Deiana Denise Sutherland

THE FOOT
OF THE
VOLCANO

MEREO
Cirencester

Mereo Books

1A The Wool Market Dyer Street Cirencester Gloucestershire GL7 2PR
An imprint of Memoirs Publishing   www.mereobooks.com

The Foot of the Volcano: 978-1-86151-620-6

First published in Great Britain in 2016
by Mereo Books, an imprint of Memoirs Publishing

Copyright ©2016

Deiana Denise Sutherland has asserted her right under the Copyright Designs and
Patents Act 1988 to be identified as the author of this work.

The address for Memoirs Publishing Group Limited can be found at
www.memoirspublishing.com

The Memoirs Publishing Group Ltd Reg. No. 7834348

The Memoirs Publishing Group supports both The Forest Stewardship Council®
(FSC®) and the PEFC® leading international forest-certification organisations. Our
books carrying both the FSC label and the PEFC® and are printed on FSC®-certified
paper. FSC® is the only forest-certification scheme supported by the leading
environmental organisations including Greenpeace. Our paper procurement policy
can be found at www.memoirspublishing.com/environment

Typeset in 11/15pt Century Schoolbook
by Wiltshire Associates Publisher Services Ltd. Printed and bound in Great Britain
by Marston Book Services Ltd, Oxfordshire

CONTENTS

Dedicated to my three children, Maria, Myron
and Merlando.

I am greatly indebted to my friends Fred Latchman, Nashatta
Durrant, Rodney Burke, Wayne Prescott, Carmel Ryan, Reginald
Isaacs, Leigh Catherine Bucks, Oscar John, Mrs Janet Sam,
Peter Beaupierre, Lucy Marshall, Jeffrey Rodgers, Joel Paris,
Roger Williams, Canute Smith and Ian Blucher, who have shown
me the meaning of true friendship, for their guidance and
sincerity. Mrs Wendy Johnson has provided encouragement and
support from an early stage of this project.

CHAPTER 1

GROWING UP

Thirty years have now come and gone since I left Dickson Village. Thirty long years, yet long as it may seem, to me it was as yesterday, for Dickson Village has remained always in my heart.

The night was cold, yet beautiful. As I walked lazily past the church towards my home, I was overwhelmed by the melodic choruses floating harmonically through the air. The giggles of lovers in the nearby lane blended beautifully with the wind as it whistled its way softly through the trees.

As I reached the top of the hill overlooking the village, an unwelcome gust of wind sent my scarf flying into the air. My legs melted beneath me as I crumbled to the ground, allowing a sense of loneliness and loss to take its toll on me, for it was on a night as cold, yet beautiful, as this that my life had been turned upside down.

I was born and grew up with my Mum in Dickson, a small village in St Vincent and the Grenadines, an idyllic volcanic Caribbean island group in the lesser Antilles. Named Hairouna (the land of the blessed) by the native Caribs, St Vincent, like its people, represents warmth and serenity. With a population of about 120,000 people the country covers about 150 square miles and consist of St Vincent, the main island, and a chain of thirty-two smaller Grenadines islands. Discovered by Columbus, St Vincent and The Grenadines gained independence from Britain in 1979, a year remembered also for the last volcanic eruption there.

Dickson is a place of unspoilt beauty, hidden on the windward side of St Vincent and the Grenadines. With a population of just two hundred people, it was to me an undiscovered paradise. The hills cascaded with lush vegetation as far as the eye could see. Hundreds of coconut trees stood tall over the village, swaying quietly with a mixture of banana and orange trees in the cool evening breeze, as the inviting stream trickled softly through them. The blended aroma of ripening fruits (mangoes, golden apples, plums, bananas, papaya etc) once in season perfumed the air. Sheer tranquillity.

In the daytime the villagers went about their chores at their own pace in the scorching sun. When it rained the street became deserted, while at night the young and old became one as the streets came alive with music, storytelling, domino playing, church crusades or simply 'liming' (Caribbean-style 'hanging-out'), weather permitting of course. It was a village where everyone knew each other and where nothing much ever happened.

Mum worked at the village shop. Every evening after school I'd play with my friend Tommy until the end of her shift, then we'd all head for home. Sometimes when the shop was empty and her back was turned Tommy and I would sneak in through the side door and help ourselves to handfuls of sweets, which we knew she'd pay for before she finished.

I had known Tommy Harrison all my life; he was my best friend. He lived across the road from me with his dad, a local man who had previously migrated to England and spent thirty years there. While there he had met and married Tommy's mum, a beautiful blue-eyed blonde called Sarah. After his many years in England, Mr Harrison had returned to Dickson with his wife. Tommy was born a year later. Unfortunately his parents separated when he was three years old, and Sarah returned to England, leaving them both behind.

Although Tommy was two years my senior, we were inseparable. He was tall, with a freckled face and full of life. I lived in his shadow. To me, he was simply the best; we shared secrets and wild, wild dreams. Mum always said that we were living in a world of our own.

As we grew older we became closer and closer; I

was the little sister he had never had. A few of the adults in the village complained, for it was the norm that children should be seen playing with children of the same sex, but our special friendship blossomed; it was different.

I never knew my father; I was told that he had died in a car crash before my birth. We had no other relatives that I knew of and my mother never remarried. I can recall vaguely, when I was about ten, asking Mum to tell me everything I needed to know about my dad. She hesitated for a moment, rested her hands gently on my shoulder, smiled faintly, then walked away. Although I was ten years old, I can remember feeling a great sense of pity, for it suddenly dawned on me that true love never dies. His memory caused her such great sorrow. Realizing this I quickly followed her into the kitchen, comforted her with a huge hug, then apologized. From that day forth Percy Steinford's name was consigned to silence.

As the years went on, not only was she my mum but my closest and dearest friend. Every evening after supper we'd sit in the old shed under the big golden apple tree a few yards from the house and she'd watch in silence as Tommy and I did our homework. The old shed was a very special place to all three of us.

On my tenth birthday Tommy presented me with a small blue box wrapped carefully in white lace tied neatly into a bow. Excitedly I opened the box and was confronted with a beautiful black wristband bearing the inscription of my name. 'Oh Tommy, it's beautiful!' I cried, admiring it carefully. He smiled and replied

'I'm really pleased you like it.'

I put my hand out and watched in silence as he took the wristband and placed it neatly around my left wrist. His hands trembled as he gazed into my eyes, 'For you, Natalie Steinford,' he mumbled, 'best friends forever.' The world stopped revolving around us. There was complete silence and in the stillness our lips met - only for a brief second. I opened my eyes, looked back and, as I thought, there stood Mum and Mr Harrison on the veranda looking at us.

We spent the remainder of the evening at the cinema and later that night, as I lay in bed unable to sleep, I reflected radiantly on my first kiss, the kiss that we both agreed the next day had never happened.

CHAPTER 2

CONVENT LIFE

I was now twelve years old, while Tommy was fourteen and attending North Union Secondary School. It was time for me to say goodbye to the rest of the village. I was going to a private secondary convent school for girls miles away.

Parting was such great sorrow. The night before I left, Tommy and I sat in the old shed all alone. We joked about the past, about the good times and the bad times we had had together. Then we vowed that we should remain friends forever. As we parted, he took hold of my hand and whispered quickly and softly, 'I love you Natalie,' and with that he ran hastily towards his home. I watched in sorrow as he disappeared inside and closed the door behind him. 'I love you too Tommy,'

I murmured. I knew he couldn't hear me - not that he needed to, for deep in his heart I believe he already knew.

As soon as I closed my eyes it was time to open them again; it was morning. I was awoken by a huge bang on the door, which was followed by mother's loud morning call, and before long, I was dressed and ready to leave. As I said my goodbyes to the rest of the village, Tommy was nowhere to be seen.

'Where's Tommy?' Mum asked.

'I haven't seen him,' replied Mr Harrison. My heart began to ache, for I could not leave without seeing him. 'Where is he?' I asked myself over and over again.

The villagers were extremely excited to see me off. They showered me with hugs and kisses. I forced many broad smiles as I scanned the group looking for Tommy. Where was he?

'Natalie, would you like to find Tommy before you leave?' Mum interrupted.

'No!' I snapped as I escaped to the car. I was now feeling angry, because I was leaving and Tommy never came to say goodbye.

Slowly we drove off, leaving the villagers behind shouting their good lucks. Quietly we drove through the village, and as we drove past Valley River I looked up and there sat Tommy on a huge rock above the river, feet dangling in the warm water, a wicker basket on his lap. He sat watching the water run lazily by. He was going to catch crayfish, something he did without fail every Saturday, his so-called alone time. I was suddenly overpowered by a sense of sadness. I felt sad,

sad that I was leaving, sad to see the look upon his face and sad to see the glistening tears running slowly down his freckled face. 'Tommy,' I whispered softly, as I too began to cry.

'Should I stop?' asked Mum.

'No,' I gasped, as I tried to fight back the tears. I waved goodbye and he managed a faint, shy smile. I watched his lips part as he said 'Bye.' Before I could reply, the car had swerved around the corner, leaving me alone and feeling terribly sad.

As we drove up to the gate of the big, old boarding school, I completely broke down. 'I can't believe I'm going to be here for the next five years,' I cried.

'Yes dear,' Mum choked, fighting back her own tears. 'You'll get through it. Please be good and work hard.'

'I promise I will Mum, I do.'

'Take good care of yourself.' We embraced. 'Everything is going to be all right,' Mum whispered.

'I love you, Mum, I love you!' I cried, as I held her tight and fought hard to stifle the tears.

Mum stayed until I was settled; then she was gone. I felt nostalgic straight away, for I had never been away from home.

I hated that dreary old school. The lights had to be out by eight and as I lay in bed at night I listened in fright as the nuns dragged their long black gowns up and down the halls during inspection. This place to me was Ghostville. I found it difficult settling into my new-found home. I missed Dickson terribly and most of all, I missed Mum and her cooking. I began by phoning her twice or more per day, for she too was finding it difficult. All my life we had never been apart. As the days turned into weeks, I missed her more and more. Tommy kept me informed with the goings-on of the village, which wasn't much, but just hearing him speak of Dickson was satisfying.

Eventually I got used to my new surroundings and settled in. I participated in every activity, joined the choir, excelled in my subjects and even joined the netball team, which was challenging but great fun. Convent life was wonderful.

At age thirteen more and more girls came to the convent and it was then that we began to share rooms. I detested the thought of having a roommate, for it was something I had never done before. One afternoon as I sat in my dorm revising, there was a knock on the door. I quickly opened it and was introduced to my new roommate, Betty, by Sister Mary. I was lost for words, for Betty wasn't what I was expecting. She was absolutely beautiful, charming and naturally friendly. Her long black hair ran in soft curls down her back like a flowing stream, her dazzling white teeth glinted in the dim light and her big brown eyes sparkled with excitement. Never before had I seen such a radiant beauty.

'Hello, I'm Betty Jackson,' she said cheerfully, extending her long arms. Our hands met.

'I'm Natalie Steinford,' I replied, 'Pleased to meet you.' We looked at each other and laughed loudly for no reason, which left Sister Mary baffled, and from that moment I felt at ease, for I knew that our friendship was going to be wonderful and special.

I helped Betty to settle, and in less than a week we knew everything there was to know about each other. She came from a family for which she held undying love; her ambition was to become a fashion designer, marry for love and have twelve children. I told her about my village and about Mum and Tommy.

As time went on our friendship grew closer and it was then that I realized how influential friends could be. I began smoking and drinking on the odd occasion; where Betty got the cigarettes and alcohol I never asked. I eventually reduced the number of calls made to Mum and found myself too busy to open or reply to Tommy's letters. I now had a new best friend.

One night we decided to transform ourselves from little convent girls into (we hoped) beautiful young women. After inspection, we sneaked out through our bedroom window, hopped on a bus and went clubbing in Kingstown, the capital, where we had the time of our lives. Because of our height and the way we dressed, no one suspected for a second that we were under age. I enjoyed every moment of it.

But as we crept slowly down the hall on our return around 5 am, an angry Sister Catherine stopped us in our tracks. 'Well, well, well,' she yelled,' 'My office, now!'

Betty was speechless and I immediately burst into tears. 'I'm so sorry, Sister Catherine,' I sobbed, 'I'm really sorry!'

'To my office, now!' she yelled once again. By this

time all the other girls were looking out of their dorms. As we turned towards the office there was a splatter as the contents of Betty's stomach hit the floor.

'Clean that up now, Natalie!' Sister Catherine shouted at me, as she turned with Betty towards our dorm, 'Report to my office at eight o'clock sharp. And to your rooms the rest of you,' she continued to yell, 'the show is now over!'

'Yes Sister,' I whispered, as I headed towards the cleaning cupboard for the mop and bucket. Betty and I lay speechless side by side, for we knew what was in store for us later.

Quite soon our parents were called and as we expected, we were both suspended for two weeks. Mum was devastated. We drove back to Dickson in complete silence. The news had already reached the village by the time we got there. There was no one waiting to greet me with open arms; they all looked at me with utter disappointment. I felt so ashamed. Not only had I let Mum and myself down, in the eyes of the villagers I was a disappointment to the whole of Dickson Village.

After a lovely supper of breadfruit and roasted salt fish with homemade coconut oil, I went to my room. I was asleep before my head touched my pillow.

Some hours later, a familiar chorus floating softly through the bedroom window awoke me. I followed the song to the old shed under the big golden apple tree, and there was Mum. It was then that I noticed how much she had changed; she now had a few strands of grey hair, which I thought suited her. She had also gained a bit of weight. The tears flowed as I saw the sadness upon her face.

'Hello Mum,' I interrupted as I flew into her open arms. We cried and hugged for what I thought was an eternity.

'It's all right,' she cried as she ran her fingers through my short black hair. I looked at my puffy brown eyes in the opposite mirror and suddenly the bumps on my brown skin began to rise and my short legs became jelly-like beneath me. I broke away from Mum, ran quickly towards the window and flung it open in search of Tommy.

'Tommy, Tommy!' I bellowed, 'Tommy!' But there was no reply. He was nowhere to be seen. 'Where's Tommy,' I asked, 'Didn't you tell him I was coming home?'

'I'm sorry dear,' Mum replied, 'But Tommy left Dickson Village six months ago.'

'Left! What do you mean he's left? Where has he gone?'

'He went to live with his mum in England. Mr Harrison died and after that he had nothing else here to stay for.'

'Died! Mr Harrison died? I interrupted. 'Why wasn't I told? Why?' I screamed.

'I'm sorry but Tommy asked me not to tell you. We didn't want to upset you.'

'Mum, he needed me and I wasn't there for him,' I replied. With those words I ran across the road until I came to Tommy's house. I threw myself down on the front porch and I cried and cried. I'd failed my best friend. The only time in his life that he had needed me I wasn't there. 'I'm sorry Tommy, I'm so sorry!' I continued to cry.

That night I found it impossible to sleep. It had been so long since I had last seen Tommy; I tried hard to imagine what he now might look like. I began to unpack.

It was then that I came across a black wristband bearing the inscription of my name. I picked it up gently, threw myself down on the bed, closed my eyes, pressed it firmly against my cheeks and in silence I remembered the night it had been given to me. 'Oh Tommy,' I whispered, as I dozed off to sleep, completely exhausted.

I returned to school and to my surprise found that Betty and I were to be separated. Despite this, our friendship continued. I headed for my new room and, finally, after what seemed to be forever, I found what I was searching for, Tommy's letters, all fifty-three of them, placed neatly at the bottom of my belongings. With haste I flung myself to the ground, sat upright back against my bed, tore open the envelopes and read them one by one. Happiness overpowered me, for the letters, as I expected, were comforting and fulfilling. I wasted no time replying.

At seventeen I graduated with some good O levels and gained my Caribbean Examination Councils certificate. On my graduation day mum was extremely proud. I was only partly happy, for all my thoughts were still centred on Tommy. During the entire ceremony my eyes were fixed on the door; I was expecting him to walk in. When we concluded and he didn't show, I couldn't fight back the build-up of tears.

'Are you OK, Natalie?' Mum asked, as I joined her.

'Overjoyed,' I lied.

Later we joined Betty and her family for celebrations at a restaurant nearby. Halfway through the celebrations Mum presented me with a small gift, neatly and colourfully wrapped. I immediately opened it. It contained a golden necklace and heart pendant and engraved at the back was 'To Natalie, love always, Mum.'

Slowly I opened the pendant. It contained a photograph of Mum, Tommy and me, taken a few days before I had left Dickson Village.

'This is beautiful. Thank you Mum,' I said. I leaned over and we cuddled.

'I've got something else for you,' she whispered, as we broke loose.

'What is it?' I said. I watched as she slowly opened her handbag and handed me a letter. Trembling, I realized it was from England, and I recognized the handwriting. The heat of the moment was unbearable as I stood up and screamed, 'Oh my god, it's from Tommy!'

Suddenly there was silence; slowly I turned around and all eyes in the entire restaurant were centred on me. 'May I be excused?' I squeaked, as I rushed from the restaurant into the dewy night. The letter was quickly opened and I began to read it carefully.

Dear Natalie,

Thanks for your letter. Words cannot express the joy I felt hearing from you again. Everything has worked out perfectly for me here in England. Mum is wonderful and thinks the world of me, she spoils me rotten. I am now in my last year of university after which I will be doing a degree in medicine. I will be coming home to St Vincent on the 9th of this month for a few weeks as I've got some business to finalise.

Natalie, I remember when we were kids how I used to look down from my window and see your smiling face looking up at me, your brown skin shining in the sun and your eyes burning like fire inviting adventure. I miss you and can't wait to see you again.

Love always,
Tommy

He was coming home! I threw myself to the ground. Oh how I longed to see him, for I had so much to tell.

'Natalie, Natalie, are you all right?' Betty shouted from behind me.

'Oh Betty,' I cried, 'He's coming home, Tommy's coming home!'

CHAPTER 3

TOMMY'S RETURN

I settled back into village life; it was three days before Tommy's arrival. The entire village waited in anticipation. I counted every minute and every second, for I couldn't wait for our reunion. Mum arranged to collect Tommy from the airport and I eagerly agreed to accompany her. On the day before his arrival I went to his old house and, with the help of a few of the villagers, we gave it a much-needed spring clean. It was now perfect. We then arranged a surprise party for him at our house.

On the way to the airport I was a nervous wreck. What was I to say to Tommy after so many years? Would he be the same, or had he changed completely? I tormented myself with question after question all the way to the airport. As we parked the car, I was motionless, almost breathless and shook like a leaf.

'Come on,' Mum said, 'Pull yourself together.' I took a deep, deep breath, tidied my face, then with pulsating heart we entered the airport. About ten minutes later we listened as the arrival of Flight 207 was announced.

'Come on, Mum!' I shouted, pulling her towards the arrival lounge. Anxiously we watched as passengers came forth one by one some twenty minutes later. The palms of my hands were wet and I was certain that the people surrounding me could count the beats of my heart.

Then suddenly the large doors opened and there he was. Well-dressed, tall and handsome, he paused and looked around.

'Tommy, Tommy!' I screamed as I fought my way through the crowd. I rushed into his arms and cried for joy. 'Oh, how I missed you!' I cried.

'I've missed you too, Natalie,' his voice, now deep and manly, replied.

We stood still holding each other for a long time. Then a familiar voice interrupted, 'Hello Tommy.'

Together we turned towards Mum. Her eyes were red, for she too had been crying. 'Mrs Steinford,' Tommy laughed, 'It's wonderful to see you again.' He broke away from me and happily I watched as they embraced.

On the way back to Dickson Village, Tommy and I had so much to talk about. He told me all about his life in England and was pleased to say that he was now a medical student. We chatted non-stop. Then mum shouted 'We're home.' Tommy took hold of my hand, and I shivered as I looked into his eyes. An unusual feeling took hold of me; it was a feeling I had never experienced before. The car halted and Tommy stepped out, still holding my hand. He turned and looked nostalgically around. 'Dickson Village, sweet old Dickson Village at last,' he murmured happily.

Mum turned the front door key and, as we walked towards the front room, I put the light on and what seemed like half the village shouted, 'Welcome home, Tommy!' There was excitement in the air. Tommy was speechless; the villagers rushed towards him and showered him with hugs and kisses. I knew he was going to be occupied for a while, so I let go of his hold on me and headed for the old shed. The party was in full swing.

I listened as 'welcome home' chantings rose high above the roof tops. Tired, I dozed off. there was a knock on the door. I opened my eyes and watched as Tommy entered the shed. Powerful and strong he stood looking down at me.

'I thought I would find you here,' he whispered. I rose and tried to get up. 'Don't,' he said as he sat down beside me. He gently took hold of my hand and again I shivered – that unusual feeling was once again taking its toll on me.

'I'm sorry Tommy,' I muttered, jumping hurriedly to my feet, 'we must join the rest of the party.'

'What sort of party will it be if the main guest is missing?'

I smiled, putting my hand forth in an effort to pull him to his feet. Athletic as he was, my effort failed and he pulled me towards him. I landed on his chest and we laughed.

'You're right,' he said, ruffling my hair.

'Stop that!' I said as we rose together.

'Catch me if you can!' he shouted as he hit me on the shoulder and ran from the shed towards the house. I stood at the door of the shed watching as he disappeared. 'Welcome home Tommy,' I smiled whole-heartedly as I ran after him.

It was absolutely wonderful to have Tommy home. Everywhere he went I followed closely in his footsteps. We were both grown up and wanted different things in life, but the childishness in us lingered still. Together we scaled the mountains and crossed the fields just as we had when we were kids. I chased him playfully through countless banana fields. Every moment spent together was truly accounted for.

Tommy decided to stay with us; it was great sleeping across the hall from him. At nights I'd listen as his snores forced their way beneath the door and into my room. His father's house was placed on the market for sale, as he had no immediate intention of returning permanently to Dickson Village. This saddened me.

Into the second week I received a telephone call from Betty and I invited her to meet Tommy. On the way to collect her from the bus station, I once again explained everything I knew about her to Tommy. I was excited at the thought of having all the three people I loved more than life itself under one roof.

We arrived at the station a few minutes late. Betty sat on her suitcase waiting anxiously. She gazed, lost, at everyone who walked by.

'Betty!' I shouted as we got close to her. Quickly she turned, rose and with a broad smile and open arms shouted, 'Hello Natalie.'

We hugged each other and laughed happily. 'So,' she gasped, 'this must be Tommy.'

'Oh Betty, I'm so sorry,' I smiled. 'Yes, this is Tommy.' I took his hand. 'Tommy, this is Betty.'

Betty extended her long arm, took his hand and said 'Hi Tommy, pleased to finally meet you. I've heard so much about you.'

'All good things, I hope,' Tommy replied shyly. She let go of his hand and I watched as their eyes slyly examined each other.

On the way back home Betty fell asleep, tired after her journey.

'She seems very nice,' Tommy whispered to me, smiling.

'She is,' I replied.

After supper Betty went straight to bed and Tommy and I went for a walk. It was a wet night, but beautiful, as we walked arm in arm silently through the village, which was deserted due to the showers of rain that had fallen earlier.

'Oh how I missed this old place,' Tommy said as he took a deep breath and inhaled the cool night air. 'It's still so green and unspoilt after all these years.' He turned and pulled me close.

'Good evening Tommy, good evening, Natalie,' interrupted one of the villagers as he appeared from nowhere and walked lazily past. 'Good evening Mr James,' we chorused. We laughed and headed for home.

The following day Betty was up early, and Tommy and I took her for a grand tour around the village. She was enjoying every moment, most of all Tommy's company. I had a very sad feeling, for the attraction they had for each other was obvious. They chased each other up the hill towards top Dickson and Betty's laughter echoed loudly through the village. Gasping for breath, I finally caught up with them. My heart ached with jealousy.

'I think we should call it a day,' I commented sharply.

'Don't be a spoilsport,' Betty laughed. 'Come on, Natalie, relax.'

'I'm very tired,' I replied. 'I'll head home.'

'Natalie,' interrupted Tommy, 'you go on home and we'll catch up with you later.'

'Are you sure?' I blurted out, confused.

'Yes,' Betty said, 'we'll be OK.'

'See you later then,' I said as I wandered down the hill towards my home.

I arrived there in tears, wiped my eyes and sat on the front porch waiting anxiously for their return. I sat there for a long time eyes, cast down on the road. Slowly the minutes mounted agonizingly into many tearful hours. Annoyed I rose and headed for the kitchen.

Then I heard a familiar laugh – Betty's. I looked out of the window and there they stood arm in arm looking happily at each other. Anger and rage took hold of me as I watched them in amazement. I went storming to my bedroom and threw myself down on the bed, closed my eyes and pretended to be asleep.

A few minutes later there was a knock, the door slowly opened, and Tommy's voice whispered 'Natalie?'

I maintained my position. The door closed softly and once again I was upset and alone.

I awoke the following day to find the house empty. There was a note from Mum saying she would be out for the rest of the day. There was no sign of Betty and Tommy. Where could they be? It was Betty's last day in Dickson. I suddenly felt happy at this thought. I was happy that she was leaving, for I wanted Tommy all to myself.

Suddenly, however, they arrived and Betty's laughter filled the room. 'Good morning, Natalie,' Tommy said as he followed Betty into the kitchen.

'Morning, guys,' I whispered as I followed slowly behind them.

We discussed our plans for the day and then Tommy said 'How about coming to the cinema later, Betty?'

'The cinema,' I butted in, 'that sounds like fun. What time are we going?'

'About four o'clock.'

'Great,' I replied as I walked off. I spent the remainder of the morning avoiding Betty and Tommy, for I didn't want to give them any excuse to be angry with me. I was determined to accompany them to the cinema.

We had an early supper with Mum, as we were expected back late. The meal was eaten in complete silence – strained silence. 'What's going on?' Mum asked, but there was no reply.

I sulked all the way to the pictures as Tommy and Betty skipped along happily beside me arm in arm. The film started and ended in what seemed to be a few seconds. What film was it? I do not know, for my mind was far, far away. We arrived back home and I dozed off, exhausted.

I was awoken by Betty's laughter, and slowly I drew the curtain and looked down. They were walking towards the house. Betty looked very happy as she swung Tommy's hand to and fro. Where had they been now?

They entered the house and I quickly joined them. 'Where have you two been?' I asked.

'For a walk,' Betty replied. 'Fancy a glass of Mauby?' she continued, heading for the kitchen.

'Yes please,' Tommy and I chorused. We looked at each other and laughter filled the room. Betty joined us and together we gave each other a much-needed group hug. 'That's better,' Mum said upon entry.

Together we all continued to laugh. 'Now let's have some fun,' Tommy shouted as he headed towards the stereo. Alston Becket Cyrus echoed through the house: *'Ah love me St Vincent, me sweet little island St. Vincent, the home of the blessed St Vincent. St Vincent,*

St Vincent I lovvvvvvve you,' we chorused as the music blasted its way through the house.

'Goodnight all!' Mum shouted. 'Goodnight!' we all screamed in reply.

We danced the night away. Then Betty said she was tired and excused herself as she also had to prepare for her journey home the following day. Tommy turned the music off. Then together we sat on the front porch. Soon I began to feel ashamed as I recalled my behaviour. As if reading my thoughts, he said softly with a shy smile 'Do I detect a hint of jealousy?'

'No,' I lied. 'Dream on.'

'If you were jealous, you should know that there is no reason to be.'

'I know that,' I managed to murmur. His hands gently touched my shoulder and I shook with pleasure as I turned to face him.

'I love you, Tommy Harrison,' I whispered softly.

'I love you too, Natalie Steinford,' he replied, 'and I always will.'

With that we said our goodnights, and for the first time since his arrival I wasn't awake to hear him snore.

Betty left the next day and I was very happy that I finally had Tommy all to myself. I wanted to make the most of our last few days together. And as I wanted, we spent each day in each other's company.

Then suddenly it was time for him to leave. This saddened me. On the night before he left, a few of the villagers gathered at our house to say their goodbyes.

Was this to be ours? I found myself in the shed alone, once again feeling very sad. I sat down, and soon Tommy entered.

'Are you trying to hide from me?' he whispered. I rose and tried to get up.

'Don't,' he said as he sat down beside me. He gently took hold of my hand and again I shivered – that unusual feeling was once again taking its toll on me. I lowered my head and tried to avoid his gaze. His hands touched my chin as he tenderly lifted my head upwards. Our eyes met, and the world stood still. Our lips touched as if guided by God into a kiss. Hungrily and passionately we kissed, as I lay prostrate on the cardboard-covered floor. He covered me with his athletic, young and powerful body.

'What are we doing?' he questioned.

'Ssh,' I whispered. His hands felt as cold as ice as they first started to caress my heaving, heated breast, but they soon warmed to their passionate task. I cried out in the wonder of excitement for I needed more - to give more. As he lifted my dress slowly over my head, my heart raced. I hurriedly undid the buttons of his shirt and my hands searched the animal nakedness of his body. The voices of the happy villagers inside grew fainter and fainter as our bodies got closer and became one.

'Natalie, I love you,' he murmured, and his lips touched my breast. I groaned in anticipation as he entered me with patient skill. I sank my fingers firmly into his back. 'Take me!' I choked, as I tried to fight back the tears of passion and give myself completely to him.

In that old shed on that beautiful evening I lost my virginity and it felt right, because it was to the man I loved more than life itself.

Finally it was time for him to leave. We drove to the airport in silence. 'How are you two doing?' Mum asked, looking at us in her rear view mirror. 'We're fine,' I managed to reply.

Tommy snuggled up to me and we maintained our position until we arrived at the airport. 'Here we are,' Mum shouted as she tried to park the car.

I watched as Tommy steadied himself and in silence we entered the airport. We arrived minutes before check in. He turned to Mum. 'Thank you, Mrs Steinford,' he whispered, 'thanks a million for everything.'

'You're welcome, dear,' she replied as she took him into her arms. 'Do take great care, and give my love to your mum.'

'I will,' he replied. He let go of her and turned towards me, taking hold of both my hands. He stared deep into my eyes and my entire body shook as the tears began to flow.

'I'll be in the café, Natalie,' Mum tactfully whispered.

Tommy lifted his hand and began to slowly wipe my tears. 'Don't cry,' he gulped, fighting hard to keep back his own tears. 'This is not the end. It's the beginning.'

'I'm sorry,' I cried.

'I love you, Natalie,' he continued. 'I always did and I always will. I've got to go now. I'll phone you as soon as I arrive.'

I was speechless. His lips gently touched mine and we kissed. Words could not express the hurt in my heart.

'Goodbye Natalie,' he said as he released my hands, kissed me once again and then turned towards the departure gate.

Motionless I watched as he walked away from me. Before he was gone I found myself yelling, to my own surprise, 'I love you, Tommy, I love you!'

'I love you too, Natalie,' he replied from afar, and then he was gone.

I entered the café as Mum was about to take the first bite of her newly-purchased roti. She turned and looked at me. Seeing how upset I was, she jumped from her chair and walked towards me.

'Come on dear,' she whispered, as she put her arms around my shoulders and led me directly to the car, which took me home through a torrent of turmoil and tears.

CHAPTER 4

THE PREGNANCY

Once again I had to adjust to life in Dickson Village without Tommy. My entire body ached for him, but he was now many miles away. We kept in regular contact by phone and the more I spoke to him the more my heart cried out – love must bring us together!

I started my new job as a secretary for a finance company a few miles away from home. This kept me pretty much occupied, but Tommy continued to linger in my mind and in my heart.

Six weeks had now passed since he had left and I was now into my job for the fifth week. 'Natalie, Natalie you're going to be late for work dear,' A familiar voice called one morning. Half asleep I crawled out of bed.

'Morning Mum,' I managed, as I raced for the bathroom.

'Natalie honey?' Mum asked, concerned, as she followed closely behind me.

'Yes,' I replied as I buried my head deeper and deeper into the toilet bowl and brought up the contents of whatever remained in my stomach. My entire body shivered, I felt exhausted and nauseated. 'Oh Mum!' I cried as I reached for some tissue. Then I was sick for the third time.

'Whatever is the matter?' a worried mum asked, as she softly began wiping away the sweat from my brow. 'Should I take you to the hospital?'

'No Mum,' I whispered, rising and splashing my face with some ice-cold water, 'I'll be fine.'

'Should I fix you some breakfast?'

'No thanks.' I dried my face and crawled slowly back towards my bed.

I telephoned in sick that day, for I would have found it impossible to work. I was scared, very scared, for deep down I knew what the problem was. I prayed that my suspicion would be false. Unfortunately, a few days later, as I had showed no signs of improvement, I was forced to see my doctor and was told that I was indeed pregnant. I was expecting Tommy's baby.

My world turned upside down and I burst into tears. I was only eighteen years old and just at the beginning of my career. I was not ready for a baby. What was I going to do? I asked myself that over and over again as I drove slowly home, bewitched, bothered and bewildered.

I arrived home in a torrent of tears. I parked the car at the bottom of the street and sat there for what seemed like hours, wondering how I was going to break the news to Mum. My house was visible from where I was, in fact it was only a few yards away.

Suddenly the car door opened and Mum sat down beside me. Handing me some tissues, she whispered calmly, 'You're pregnant, aren't you?'

I couldn't reply, for shame wouldn't allow me.

'How far gone are you?' she asked.

'Six weeks,' I managed to reply.

'Well, there's no point in you sitting here feeling sorry for yourself. The damage is already done.'

'What am I going to do, Mum?' I cried, 'What am I going to do?'

Before she could reply the phone rang and she raced from the car into the direction of the house. Slowly I followed her.

'Tommy's on the phone, Natalie,' she shouted from the window.

'Tell him I'm not in,' I whispered, as the tears began to give way once again. I ran into the house, slamming the door behind me. I arrived in the front room and threw myself down on the settee. Mum joined me a few seconds later and I buried myself into her comforting arms.

'Tommy says he'll call again later,' she whispered. I did not reply. 'You've got to let him know, Natalie. He is the father after all,' she continued.

'I just need some time to think things through, Mum,' I replied.

'OK then, dear.' She smiled, stroking my hair. 'Whatever you decide to do, remember I'm with you all the way.'

'Thanks Mum,' I whispered. I rose and crept up the stairs towards my room.

'Try and get some sleep,' she called from behind me, 'I'll bring you up something to eat in about an hour's time.'

'Thanks Mum, see you later,' I replied with a faint smile. I had always known my mum was marvellous.

The following day at work I found it impossible to concentrate, as I was very confused. On the way back home later that evening, I parked the car at the village shop and it was then that I realized that the news of my pregnancy was already around the village. Most of the villagers were strict Catholic, and sex outside marriage was not allowed. Ignorant villagers looked at me in scorn, close friends refused to speak to me and everywhere I went small groups of immature lads sneered and made funny comments. I felt betrayed and dirty.

Mum took it all rather well. She ignored all the gossips and dirty remarks. This really did upset me, for it was unfair that my mum should be blamed for my wrongdoings.

The next day I went to the doctor and decided to have an abortion. As I was a Catholic, this was forbidden, but I didn't care, for I had already broken the rules. Tommy knew nothing about my situation, for I refused to take his calls, which he made quite frequently. Of course Mum strongly disagreed with me, but in the end she accepted my decision.

It was soon the day of the abortion. On the way to the hospital Mum asked, 'Are you all right, dear?'

'Yes,' I replied, as I sank back into my seat hoping it would devour me. I closed my eyes and remembered Tommy. *This abortion has to be*, the voice inside me whispered. Tommy and I were both young and had our entire lives and careers ahead of us. The abortion had to happen.

Slowly I drifted back to the night Tommy and I had made love. Back I went to the last two weeks we spent together before he returned to England... back I went to our first kiss... to our goodbye at the airport... to his declaration of love for me...

'Natalie, we're here,' Mum interrupted. I opened my eyes, adjusted myself and sighed. Mum rested her hands on my knee, looked at me and asked, 'Are you sure you're doing the right thing?'

'Yes I am,' I replied. 'It's for the best.'

'The best for who?' I made no reply.

As we entered the hospital I felt scared. I squeezed Mum's hand tightly, took a deep breath and whispered to myself, 'Please Lord, tell me this is all a dream.'

'Everything's going to be fine,' Mum said comfortingly. As I looked at her the tears came once again, for she was simply the best. She had such great strength.

'I love you Mum!' I cried as we headed towards the reception area. She looked at me and smiled another comforting smile.

Fifteen minutes later, I was admitted to the ward, and Mum sat closely by my bedside. As I lay in the hospital bed, a great sense of sadness suddenly overpowered me as I finally realized that it wasn't a dream after all, this was reality. I was scared; the tears flowed once again as Mum took hold of my hand in an effort to console me.

The doctor and nurses arrived, introduced themselves and began making preparations, and then once again my mind began to travel. I flashed back to the many wonderful times Tommy and I had had together, from childhood upwards. Sadness overpowered me as I thought about what I was about to do. I was about to destroy our unborn child, the child of the man I loved.

Suddenly, as if guided by an unknown presence, I leapt from the bed, pushed my way past the nurses and doctor surrounding me and raced from the room towards the car park, where Mum finally caught up with me. I threw myself into her arms and cried for joy. For the first time in weeks I felt happy - happy that a part of Tommy was now growing inside me and feeling confident to face the future whatever it brought.

As we arrived home and began to leave the car I turned to Mum and said 'I'm going for a walk through the village.'

'Are you sure that's a good idea?'

'Yes,' I answered as I turned and headed out. Head held high, I strolled through the village. 'Good afternoon.' I shouted at everyone that passed me by. I grinned widely, for I was so happy - happy that a part of Tommy was going to be with me forever. Would it be a little girl or boy? Only time would tell.

The weeks dragged slowly by. One day on my return from work the phone rang and I picked it up. 'Hello Natalie!' The voice on the other end said joyfully. It was Tommy. He was overwhelmed to hear my voice, and I his.

I acted as normally as I possibly could. Then, unfortunately, I lied. I said I had met someone else and that I believed that a long-distance relationship wouldn't work. This broke my heart as much as it broke his. As I hung up the phone, I cried and cried, for I couldn't believe what I had done. In less than a minute, I had broken two hearts which should have been beating as one, Tommy's and mine.

Tommy continued to call and sent letters. I remained strong, for I thought I was doing what was best; I wanted him to finish his studies and graduate as Dr Tommy Harrison. I smiled at this thought. I didn't reply to any of his letters and eventually he gave up. I read every one, then placed them carefully in an old trunk under my bed. His words were always so comforting and encouraging.

My stomach grew larger and larger, and as the months went by I became happier, for our child was on his or her way.

As I expected, Mum stood by me all the way. She attended antenatal classes with me and surprisingly decorated the spare room all by herself for baby's arrival, creating a gorgeous nursery. Sometimes I'd wonder what life would have been like without her. She was a real angel.

One morning on my way to work, I noticed an old Volvo parked outside Tommy's old house. I looked up and saw that the upstairs windows were open and for curiosity's sake I parked my car behind the red Volvo and walked carefully up the stairs and knocked on the door. A few seconds later a woman who looked to be in her early fifties appeared, smiling at me. 'Hello,' I said, extending my hand. 'I'm Natalie. I live across the road.'

'Hello Natalie,' she replied. I'm Mrs Rhodes, pleased to meet you, do come in.'

I entered the house and followed her into the empty front room. 'I'm just getting the house ready for my son Peter,' she said, 'He'll be moving in on Saturday.'

'Will he be living here alone?' I asked inquisitively.

'Yes, she replied. 'He's just divorced and fancied a new start. I see you're expecting.' She nodded towards my stomach. 'How far gone are you?'

'Seven months,' I replied softly with a shy smile.

'Is this your first?' she asked.

'Yes.'

'Your husband must be overjoyed,' she said, looking at my wedding finger. But it was bare.

'I'm sorry Mrs Rhodes,' I interrupted, 'I've got to go now. I'm on my way to work.'

'I'm ever so sorry dear,' she smiled, leading me to the door. 'Please feel free to call in anytime.'

'Goodbye Mrs Rhodes,' I said. 'It was a pleasure meeting you.'

I shook her hand gently and headed for my car. I

watched in my rear view mirror as she stood at the top of the steps waving until I was gone.

CHAPTER 5

THE HANDSOME STRANGER

The following day was my day off and, as I had nothing much to do, I decided to help Mum out at the village shop. As I was entering the shop the books I was carrying to pass time fell from my hands. Holding my back, I stooped to pick them up.

'Here, let me help you,' a man's voice whispered. Slowly I steadied myself and was confronted by a short and handsome young man. His big brown eyes sparkled as he looked up and smiled at me. I watched in complete silence as he collected the books from the floor, rose and passed them to me.

'Thank you very much,' I said as I turned to walk away.

'It was a pleasure,' he replied from behind me.

I about turned and said, 'You're not from around here, are you?'

'No,' he replied with a faint smile, and with that he said goodbye and then walked hurriedly from the shop. Astonished, I watched as he closed the door behind him. 'Come back,' the voice inside me called.

'Who was that man, Mum?' I asked, as I approached her.

'I don't know,' she replied. 'A passer-by perhaps.'

I spent the remainder of the day dreaming about that handsome, short stranger. One minute he was there, then the next he was gone. Just like the Scarlet Pimpernel.

The weeks dragged slowly on. I was now eight and a half months pregnant and on maternity leave, which I found boring. I had to keep occupied in an effort to block the memories of Tommy from my mind. I passed the time away in the old shed, which was now a sacred place to me – the place where I had lost my virginity and conceived the baby I was now carrying.

One morning I noticed that Mrs Rhodes' red Volvo was parked outside Tommy's old house. With nothing much to do, I decided to pop in. I crossed the road and headed towards the house. I knocked on the door several times, but there was no answer. I took a couple of steps backwards and looked up at the top window but couldn't see anyone.

'Mrs Rhodes!' I called loudly, 'It's Natalie.' Still there was no reply. Where could she be?

Feeling like stretching my legs, I decided to take a slow walk through the village. It was midday and very hot. The baby kicked inside me. 'How are you doing in there, little one?' I asked, clasping my hands to feel its every move. Once again it kicked as if to say 'Yes, Mum, I'm fine'. I giggled at the thought of it all and whispered to myself, not long now.

As I reached the village post office I was completely exhausted. Mum was next door at work in the general shop. Feeling thirsty, I entered the post office and bought myself a well-earned ice-cold glass of freshly-made lime juice, which I found refreshing.

'Are you OK now?' asked Cassandra, the shop assistant.

'Yes,' I replied before departing. 'Hello, Mum!' I shouted, as I entered next door.

'Hi Natalie,' she replied. 'Thought I heard you coming over.'

Before I could reply there was an electrifying pain and I cried out in agony. I gasped for breath and leaned over slightly for support on the unit in front of me. 'Are you all right?' Mum asked, as she rushed towards me. The pain struck again and I cried out in total agony. 'Can someone please call an ambulance!' Mum screamed, as she took hold of my hand and led me towards her chair.

Forty-five minutes later I was in hospital, Mum seated by my side. I reached for the glass of water opposite me, took a sip and smiled. Tommy junior was now on the way. I was a bit worried for I was a few weeks early.

My water gave way and a few minutes later I was rushed to the delivery room and on that scorching hot afternoon, I gave birth to a beautiful, healthy baby girl, Tina Steinford. The nurse passed her to me and as I took her into my arms I cried for joy. She weighed seven pounds and two ounces; she was freckle-faced with long arms and legs just like her father.

'Isn't she beautiful?' Mum cried, as I passed Tina to her. 'I can't believe it, I'm a grandmother.' She gave a hearty laugh. 'Tommy's got a right to know, Natalie,' she said, looking at me.

Suddenly I felt sad and ashamed. I turned away and the tears flowed. My thoughts drifted as I remembered Tommy's smile, the joy he would have felt on the birth of his daughter. It was a moment I knew that he would have cherished forever.

I was discharged three days later and as Mum drove past Tommy's old house, I noticed the red Volvo was still parked outside.

Mum was really proud of her new granddaughter and took pleasure in showing baby Tina off to the villagers. Although I told her not to take any time off work, she insisted and took two entire weeks off.

Early one morning there was a knock on the door.

'Are you expecting anyone?' Mum asked, as she rose from the breakfast table.

'No,' I replied. 'It's probably one of the villagers.' I watched as she opened the door and a happy and familiar voice shouted 'Hello Mrs Steinford.'

'Betty!' I screamed, as I rushed out to greet her

with a hug. 'My god, how have you been? It's been such a long time.'

'Natalie darling,' she said, as she held me tight. 'It's so wonderful to see you again. Well, where is my beautiful goddaughter?'

'Upstairs asleep,' I replied. With that she ran noisily up the stairs. 'Do try and keep the noise down,' I said, as I caught up with her. 'I've just got her off to sleep.'

We entered the nursery and stood arm in arm over Tina's cot. 'Isn't she gorgeous!' Betty gasped. 'You must be extremely proud.'

'I am,' I replied.

She turned and held me tight. 'Congratulations, darling, and well done.'

We returned to the dining room and Betty talked all through breakfast. She was so excited. As a matter of fact she was always excited – she was such a jolly, friendly person.

'I was so happy when your mum rang with news of Tina, and I just couldn't wait to see her,' she said. 'And how is Tommy? I bet he can't wait to see his little angel.'

I'm sure my expression changed, as I excused myself from the table.

'Natalie?' Betty called. I did not reply. I sat quietly on the steps, eyes looking down the road. Why did he have to leave? the voice inside questioned. If only he was here to call me, to hold me close in his arms, to whisper sweet nothings in my ear...

By the time Betty caught up with me I was in

tears. She sat down beside me and threw her arms comfortingly around me.

'Tommy doesn't know,' I whispered softly.

'Natalie how could you? Why didn't you tell him? He adores you.'

In tears I poured my heart out. 'I miss him so much, Betty,' I cried. 'What am I going to do, whatever am I going to do?' I rested my head against her shoulder and we sat in silence, complete silence.

Betty spent a week in Dickson and in that week she filled me in with all that had been going on in her life. It was great to finally catch up with her, as she was always travelling and eight out of twelve months was spent out of the country. She was now the proud owner and manager of a designer clothes store. She was single and very much enjoying it. I was so proud of her; it was always her dream to be an entrepreneur. Her dream had become reality, and for that I was extremely proud.

One evening we decided to take Tina for a walk. I noticed that the red Volvo was still parked in Tommy's drive. Mrs Rhodes hadn't had the pleasure of meeting my new pride and joy, so that day I found myself knocking on the door, but there was no answer.

'Come on, Natalie,' Betty called. 'I don't think there's anyone in.'

We headed down the road with Tina sleeping quietly in her pram.

'Well,' Betty said. 'Tell me more about this handsome stranger, the one you met at the shop.'

'There's nothing more to tell,' I replied with a shy smile.

'So it wasn't love at first sight?'

'Don't be silly,' I blushed. 'I didn't even get a chance to ask him his name.'

'Is that a sparkle in your eyes I see, Natalie Steinford?' Betty teased.

'No!' I responded with a giggle. 'Will you please drop it?'

'OK,' she laughed. 'Just one more question, do you ever think about him?'

I lowered my head and lied. 'No. Now do you mind?'

She laughed heartily and I slapped her on the arm and shouted, 'Shut up before I give you another.'

As we approached the village shop, Mum was on her way out with some groceries. 'Where are you three going?' she asked.

'Nowhere in particular,' Betty replied.

I watched as Mum placed the groceries at the bottom of Tina's pram and then took hold of the handle. Betty and I hugged and followed Mum and Tina all the way home.

As we walked pass Tommy's house, Betty shouted, 'The lights are on at Mrs Rhodes. 'Maybe she's in.'

'I'll take Tina to see her now,' I replied.

'I'll come with you,' Betty said.

'I'll go home and start the supper,' Mum said, smiling at us.

We approached the house and I knocked loudly on the door. 'Just a minute,' a man's voice responded. Seconds later, the door opened and I was speechless, for there standing before me was my stranger, the stranger I had longed for – the stranger who had lingered on my mind from the moment I had met him in the village shop; the Scarlet Pimpernel, my handsome stranger.

There was complete silence. My heart throbbed as we stared deeply into each other's eyes, forgetting that there was a world revolving around us. Someone coughed and together we looked to see who it was. Betty stood at the bottom of the stairs smiling radiantly at us. 'Isn't this romantic?' she said with a wide grin.

I blushed and turned towards my stranger with trembling arms and said, 'Hi, I'm Natalie Steinford and this is my friend Betty. We're looking for Mrs Rhodes.'

'Hello, Natalie,' he said, smiling and taking hold of my hand. 'I'm Peter Rhodes. I'm sorry, my mother isn't here at the moment.'

There was an awkward silence, and then he said, 'Do please come in.'

'I'll go and give your mum a hand with the tea,' Betty said.

'No,' replied Peter sharply. 'Do come in for a while.' Turning to me he continued, 'I see you've had the baby, Natalie.'

'Yes,' I replied. 'I've got a little girl and her name is Tina.'

'May I?' he asked as he extended his arms in an effort to take her from Betty.

'Sure you can, please do,' I replied, as he took Tina into his arms. His eyes sparkled with excitement, mingled with a gentle kindness.

'Hello gorgeous,' he said to Tina. 'I see you're nearly as pretty as your mummy.' Once again I blushed as he lifted his head and looked directly at me.

We followed him inside and I noticed that the house was already tastefully decorated and fully furnished.

'This is quite beautiful,' Betty gasped, and I had to silently agree, for it was exquisite.

'Thank you very much,' Peter replied. He led us into the front room, handed Tina to me and asked, 'Can I get any of you something to drink? Hard, soft, hot or cold?'

'Tea please,' I replied. 'White with two sugars.'

'And Betty?'

'The same,' she answered.

'That's two teas, both white. I'll see what I can do to please you,' he said before he disappeared into the kitchen.

I watched as he walked away. *Go on, follow him*, a voice inside me whispered. I fidgeted with Tina's fingers as I tried to block out the voice inside my head.

'Well,' Betty interrupted, 'he's drop dead gorgeous.'

'Is he?' I said. 'Can't say I've noticed.'

We laughed loudly together. I steadied myself and said 'My god, Betty, I'm acting like a lovesick teenager'. Which of course is exactly what I was

'But you are,' Betty teased and again we laughed. We heard Peter's footstep as he returned with the hot drinks.

'Talking about me behind my back, I suppose,' he giggled as he entered the room.

'Something like that,' remarked Betty. We all filled the room with laughter – even Tina.

We spent an hour with Peter and I got to understand that Mrs Rhodes had already returned home and was pleased to learn that he was actually living alone. As Mrs Rhodes had told me, he confirmed that he was divorced, had two children and was a doctor, and was now a valuable new addition to the Dickson Village health clinic. He talked about his past experiences, his love for his children and about the pattern of events that had led to his divorce. Betty and I listened sympathetically as a sad story unfolded, as most of them are.

'I'm sorry,' he said after a while. 'You didn't come to hear me go on about my sad past. Let's talk about something else.'

'That's OK,' Betty said, steadying herself. 'We are very good listeners.'

'I bet you are,' he said, with a smile. Turning to me he asked 'Are you married, Natalie?'

'No,' I answered quickly.

'Tina's father?'

'They separated a few months ago,' Betty interrupted, 'and he emigrated to England.'

'Yes,' I confirmed as he looked longingly at me.

'Well,' he said, clearing the coffee table, 'his loss. Anyone for another drink?'

'No thanks,' I replied. 'I think we should be going now. Time for Tina's bath.'

He walked us to the door and pleasantly showed us out. 'Thank you for coming,' he said. 'We must do this again some time.'

'It was truly a pleasure,' Betty and I said, echoing each other. We shook his hand, and I'm not quite sure whether my handshake took a little longer than it should have; maybe I imagined it, even the little squeeze that was ever so gentle. I smiled and said, 'Goodbye Peter! See you soon.'

We walked away as he stood in the doorway, silently watching. I glanced over my shoulder several times and caught his gaze - a sort of kind but sad one. We arrived home and before I closed the door behind me, I looked across the road and caught his final gaze. For the last time he waved, and so did I. Slowly Peter closed his door. A few seconds later the light went off and he emerged with car keys in hand, ready to drive to - where, I wondered? Who was he likely to meet? As his tail lights disappeared into the night, I told myself I had no right to even think like this.

For most of that night I found myself stationed at my bedroom window, lights out, eyes centred on the house across the road, anxiously awaiting Peter's return. I closed my eyes and drifted back to when I had first met him at the village shop. Then I remembered Tommy, and I felt sad. It had been a month since his last letter. Had he now given up on me?

My thoughts grew deeper and deeper. The thought of never seeing Tommy again scared me. I buried my face in the palms of my hands and whispered, 'Oh Tommy, I'm ever so sorry.' Was I really too late? How could I have such feelings for another man –the feeling that I held for Tommy I now had for someone else. Was it possible to love two men at the same time? This was going to be an impossible task, for deep down I knew that my love for Tommy could never ever die completely. I was confused.

A car came fast up the road and screeched loudly. I maintained my position. In silence I watched as Peter closed the car door behind him. He looked up and stared across the road at my house. Under the moonlight I watched as he stood looking lost and tired, but I couldn't move. He turned and headed up the steps, quickly disappearing inside. His lights went on and I rose with shaking knees and threw myself down on my bed. Soon I was fast asleep.

CHAPTER 6

THE DATE

Gradually the days turned into weeks and the weeks turned into months. Tina was growing beautifully. I returned to work. I employed Kate, a full-time childminder, to look after Tina. Kate was absolutely charming, a proud mother of two boys, married and living in Bay Road, which was in the other parish, Georgetown, about thirty minutes' walk from Dickson Village.

Happy memories of Tommy continued to linger in my mind. Though he was miles away from me, I often closed my eyes, thought hard and felt his presence near. I began to avoid Peter; the feeling I felt for him I tried hard to hide. Though I wasn't in touch with Tommy I felt as though I was betraying him, for I believed he was the only man I loved and always would. How could I have lustful feelings for another? I was afraid and ashamed.

Peter tried desperately to contact me. He left messages on the answering machine and with Mum and Kate. Sometimes he'd telephone me at work.

One evening as Kate was preparing to leave, there was a knock on the door. 'Can you get the door please, Kate?' I shouted from upstairs. After a short while, she called out, 'Natalie, Dr Rhodes is here to see you.'

The brush fell from my hand and I stood still.

'Natalie,' Kate called again, 'Are you all right?'

'Yes, Kate,' I choked. 'Please show Dr Rhodes into the front room. I'll be down shortly.'

Trembling I tried to retrieve the comb, but my skirt split at the side. 'Darn it,' I whispered, and took the skirt off, in an effort to replace it with a pair of jeans. Somehow my legs got tangled and I fell to the floor with a great bang. 'Ouch!' I cried, as I tried to get up.

'What's going on?' Kate had heard the noise, and called out from below.

'Everything's fine,' I lied.

'I'm leaving now,' she continued. 'Tina's asleep. See you tomorrow.'

'Thanks, Kate,' I replied as I tidied myself in the mirror. 'See you.'

I listened as she said goodbye to Dr Rhodes and then she was gone.

Once again I steadied myself, took a deep breath and then descended the stairs towards my uninvited guest. As I entered the front room, he rose, looked straight at me and sternly said, 'You didn't reply to any of my calls or messages, so I have decided to call in to see you in person.' Before I could reply he continued, 'Supper Saturday night, and I refuse to take no for an answer. I'll pick you up at seven thirty.' With that, he kissed me gently on the cheek, then left.

Astonished and impressed, I listened as he closed the door and ran hurriedly down the steps outside. I smiled a very happy smile.

A few days later I found myself dressed and ready at seven o'clock waiting for Peter. 'You look absolutely beautiful,' Mum gasped as she came in, Tina in hand.

'Thanks, Mum,' I whispered with a feeling of warm satisfaction.

'Give us a twirl,' she said, and I turned slowly. Her eyes sparked with excitement. 'What do you think, Tina?' she asked. Tina giggled, I believe with a sense of approval. Mum and I laughed.

Someone called from outside. 'That must be Peter,' Mum said as she went down to see. I took one last glance in the mirror, then caught up with them at the foot of the stairs.

'Hello,' I said to Peter, smiling radiantly.

'Hello,' he replied. 'These are for you.' He presented me with a fresh-picked bunch of hibiscus mixed with a few yellow buttercups.

'Peter, they're beautiful,' I cried. 'Thank you.'

'It's a pleasure,' he replied. I passed the flowers to Mum.

'Now your chariot awaits,' Peter said, extending his arm. My hand hooked his as I kissed Mum and Tina goodbye.

'Have a great time,' Mum shouted before I entered the car.

As we drove off into the early night I was happy but somehow upset, for Peter didn't mention anything about my brand new long backless baby blue silk evening dress. He made no comment on my appearance at all. This saddened me. But then, as if reading my thoughts, he turned to me and said, 'You look a million dollars.'

'Thank you,' I replied with great satisfaction.

'Go on, you're allowed to smile, you know.'

I smiled, and then it turned into laughter.

Our first date was successful. I felt relaxed with Peter. During the meal we talked about everything. I told him all about Tommy and he listened in complete silence. By the time I had finished, I was in tears. I felt relieved that I'd finally got everything off my chest.

He lifted my chin and said with a comforting smile, 'Come on, cheer up.'

'Thanks for being so honest,' he said. 'Now come on, let's dance.'

I remember asking myself as he led me towards the dance floor, how could he be so calm and understanding? The night was perfect. I remember wishing and hoping that it would never end.

We arrived home as dawn was breaking. I noticed that Mum's bedroom light was on; I smiled at the thought of her waiting up for her little girl. Peter parked the car, turned towards me and said, 'Thanks for a wonderful evening.'

'No, thank you,' I replied shyly.

He leaned over, and his lips touched mine. My heart raced as I returned his kiss passionately. His rough manly hands fumbled my neckline, and my entire body ached with heated excitement. Suddenly he stopped. 'I'm so sorry, Natalie,' he apologised, 'I'm really sorry.'

'That's OK,' I lied, for the voice inside me was pleading desperately for more. I steadied myself, then emerged from the car in a dreamlike state. Peter did likewise. He walked me up the steps.

'Thanks again for a truly wonderful evening,' I whispered before entering the house. He stroked my hair into place and I looked up into a face that was handsome, kind and gentle. Once again we kissed. Then I heard Tina's loud cry.

'Duty calls,' I said, still looking at him. 'Good morning Peter.'

'Good morning Natalie,' he answered, politely kissing me once again. 'We must do this again soon.' With that he left and I entered the house, then went up the stairs to my beautiful Tina.

It was Sunday, and I slept till late afternoon. I was awoken suddenly by a knock on the front door. 'I'll get it, Mum,' I shouted, hearing her next door with Tina. I crawled out of bed, found my slippers and dressing gown and then went down the stairs to the door. 'Peter!' I shouted, amazed. He took me into his arms and we kissed. 'Would you like to stay for supper, Peter?' Mum asked, as she joined us.

'Yes thanks, Mrs Steinford,' he replied.

From that Sunday, Peter and I became very close.

I was once again the talk of the village. We began seeing each other regularly, and slowly our friendship developed into a serious relationship. We made no effort to hide the feelings that we had for each other and as the days went on our love for each other grew stronger. He was wonderful with Tina and treated her as if she were his own. He took me to meet his family, but I thought they despised me, including Mrs Rhodes. She thought no woman was good enough for her son, especially a young single-parent Catholic girl. She constantly reminded him that he was about to make another mistake, because the breaking up of his marriage had left him totally devastated. Her attitude towards us made us stronger; we closed ranks and hoped that things would change.

CHAPTER 7

LEAVING HOME

Time quickly flew by, and months became years. Tina was growing up very fast. There wasn't a trick she missed. She reminded me of her dad in every way. I often wondered what had happened to Tommy, and sometimes when I was alone, I'd cry at the thought of never seeing him again and in silence I would close my eyes and wish him nothing but the very best.

It was soon Tina's birthday and the house was packed with screaming kids from the village. Their loud cries and laughter softened only for a brief second as Kate's strained voice made its way to the top. I was happy to see the smile on Tina's excited face as she fought hard to open her presents. She was growing up beautifully, and Tommy still knew nothing of her existence.

The party went very smoothly, and as I was escorting the last guest on their way out Peter arrived. 'You're just in time to help with the cleaning up,' I teased.

'Oh dear,' he replied and turning to the departing guest asked, 'Whatever have I let myself in for?' Together we laughed. The guest said her goodbyes and then he followed me into the kitchen.

Mum bathed an exhausted Tina and then put her to bed, while Kate, Peter and I tackled the cleaning chores. Three hours later the entire house was spotless. Mum, who joined us for the second hour, said her goodnights and retired to a well-earned slumber. Shortly after, Kate left and Peter and I were at last alone.

'My god, I'm tired,' I whispered, with a huge yawn.

'I bet you are,' Peter replied. 'Fancy a strong drink?'

'Yes please,' I answered on my way to the front room. 'Sunset rum and coke please.'

A few minutes later he joined me carrying two glasses of iced sunset rum and coke. He placed them on the coffee table and sat on the chair opposite me.

'Come here,' he said, patting his lap.'

'No, you come here,' I smiled.

'Tell me, who's the boss, you or me?' he said playfully.

'Me, of course,' I chuckled. With that he took the cushion he was resting on and threw it playfully at me. Likewise I took my cushion and threw it back at him. We began a cushion fight and as the childishness inside me gave way, I ran towards him in laughter. We wrestled and fell to the floor. I was enjoying every moment; it brought back memories of Tommy and me.

We paused and as I stroked my hair back into place, our eyes met. We kissed longingly and passionately. Then on that happy night, as I regained a sudden burst of energy, Peter and I made love for the first time. I couldn't have asked for a better way to end what turned out to be a wonderful day - a day that was truly made in heaven.

We lay side by side on the carpet, our naked, wet bodies shining brightly under the beautiful moonlight that was beaming through the windows. Peter sat upright and took a sip of his drink. I rested my head on his chest, and in silence he played with my hair.

'Can you please pass me my trousers?' he asked after a while.

'Why, you're not leaving already?'

'Are you trying to get rid of me, young lady?' he teased.

I stretched over and reached for his trousers. He smiled a happy smile as I handed them to him. I watched as he fumbled through his pockets. At last he found what he was looking for, took a deep breath, pulled me upright and asked 'Are you feeling OK?'

'Yes,' I replied with puzzled eyes. He looked at me and once again he began playing with my hair in a nervous fashion. I smiled with pleasure.

'I love you, Natalie,' he said softly. I took hold of his hand and replied, 'I know you do.' But that was my only reply, for I was still confused. The feeling I felt for him was strong, but I wasn't yet sure whether or not it was love, for I still felt something stronger for Tommy.

'I've got something for you,' he continued.

'What is it?'

He took a small jewellery box from behind him, opened it and said, 'Natalie Steinford, will you marry me?'

I was flabbergasted. Motionless, I sat staring at the huge diamond ring. This wasn't how I had imagined my proposal to be, and this wasn't the person I wanted to ask me. I cried softly.

'Natalie,' he interrupted me. My heartbeats echoed loudly across the room as if pounding rhythmically to the beat of a drum. I looked into his eyes and surprised myself as my lips parted and I said, 'Yes, I will.'

'You will!' he shouted happily. We embraced, then we kissed.

After a short while he placed the ring on my finger. Then a deep sense of sadness overpowered me as I remembered Tommy. The tears gave way as I fumbled with my wristband, given to me by Tommy.

'Are you sure you're OK?' Peter asked.

'Yes, I'm fine' I lied. 'I'm just so happy. In fact I think this is the happiest day of my whole life.'

'There's something else I would like to ask you, Natalie.'

'Well, out with it then.'

He paused and I watched carefully as he took a deep breath. His icy hands took hold of mine as he said, 'I want you and Tina to move in with me.'

I gasped, lowered my head and for the second time that night I felt sad and ashamed, for how could I move into Tommy's old house with another man? The villagers would love this. My heart ached as I conjured up in my mind all the wrongs that I had done to Tommy. Eventually I convinced myself that he was indeed better off without a bitch like me.

'Do you need some time to think about it, Natalie?' Peter tactfully asked.

'No, no!' I retorted, and without any other thought said, 'I would love to move in with you.' I forced a big smile.

He held me close and said, 'Thank you for making me the happiest man in St Vincent and the Grenadines. I love you, Natalie.'

I rested my head on his shoulder as he held me tight; in the stillness I closed my eyes and was once again deep in thought. Oh Tommy!

The following day I awoke after a sleepless night and found myself on the floor of my bedroom. I twisted my new diamond ring around and around on my finger. I couldn't explain my feelings - a mixture of happiness, sadness and confusion.

There was a knock. 'Just a minute,' I answered as I rose, steadied myself and opened the locked door. I was greeted by Mum's smiling face. Immediately I felt a sense of warmth and comfort.

'Good morning,' she said cheerfully. 'I see Hurricane Ivan has swept through my front room.'

'I'm sorry Mum,' I blushed. She came in and together we sat down on the bed. She looked at me with caring eyes, for she knew me only too well. 'Mum,' I whispered, 'Peter has asked me to marry him.'

'That's fantastic,' she said with excitement. I showed her my diamond ring and she gasped, 'Natalie, darling, it's beautiful.' We hugged as she offered her congratulations and blessings. 'Peter is a very lucky man,' she concluded.

I began to cry, and she comforted me silently. Then, as if reading my thoughts, she quietly asked 'Tommy, is that what's troubling you?'

'Of course not!' I lied. I jumped up and turned away, for I couldn't look her in the eyes. 'He has also asked me to move in with him.'

'Before marriage?' She said, shocked. I nodded my head.

'Natalie, whatever next? What would the villagers think? and into Tommy's old house as well, Natalie. Come and sit down, dear,' she pleaded.

I sat by her side and once again she hugged me. We sat quietly, for what seemed like hours. 'Now go on,' she said suddenly. 'You put the pot on and make your mother one of your lovely cups of guinea pepper tea.'

As I left she maintained her position and I could tell that she was now in deep thought. She always found a solution to any problem. I walked on.

Two weeks later I found myself packed. Tina and I were ready to move in with Peter. Some of the villagers helped with the moving of Tina's cot and a few boxes and suitcases. Mum followed close behind me and made certain that Peter's house was perfect for Tina and me to live in. Kate, who was now making herself familiar with the new surroundings, looked very sad.

That night she left, still looking sad. Mum stayed for supper, which Peter took pleasure in preparing. She later left leaving Peter, Tina and me behind. I stood on the porch looking at her, as she made her way across the street towards our house. She turned and waved at me. I smiled a faint smile as I waved and forced out a 'See you, tomorrow.' She returned my wave and disappeared inside, alone.

Streams of tears gave way as I crumpled to the ground, clutching the door handle. 'Come on,' a man's voice softly whispered. I looked up and caught full view of Peter as he knelt down beside me and then lifted me gently into his arms. As he carried me slowly up the stairs the tears continued to flow as I thought of Mum all alone. Tina and I had Peter. I drifted off to sleep full of guilt.

CHAPTER 8

THE SECRET

Tina and I gradually adapted to our new home. Peter made sure that everything was to our liking, and Mum was included in everything we did. Anything we wanted we got. We ate out regularly, shopped regularly, and life was perfect.

The years flew by; as the saying goes, time flies when you're having fun. Being with Peter was heavenly. Then, sadly, just as we were comfortable, Peter changed completely. Was I so happy that I didn't notice the change in him?

He came home often late at night with the smell of alcohol on his breath. He became very possessive, and Kate complained constantly of his flirting with her and others. We had arranged to get married before the hurricane season began in October, and although he was changing for some strange reason, I still wanted to become his wife.

'Maybe he's just scared of getting married again,' I said to Mum one evening after work.

'Remember, dear,' she replied, 'you didn't ask him to marry you, he asked you. If you're not happy, you're always welcome to come back home.'

'Thanks, Mum,' I said. She reached over and held my hand.

That night I found myself waiting anxiously for Peter's return, for deep down I knew that something was troubling him. Something he was afraid to talk to me about. Was he jealous of the relationship I had with my mum?

Then his key turned in the door and he entered the house, followed by Robert, his best friend. I watched as they both staggered into the front room, highly intoxicated and unaware of my presence on the stairs. I looked up at the clock on the wall and realised that it was now three-thirty in the morning.

As I followed them into the front room Peter saw me and shouted, 'Hello darling.' I made no effort to reply. Robert, who for some reason thought it was funny, burst into laughter, 'Be quiet,' I begged, 'You'll wake Tina.' Peter then put his finger to his lips and said, 'Ssh.' Robert laughed uncontrollably. Peter staggered towards me. I sat down as he landed on my lap. He kissed me and politely I returned his kiss. Robert was now asleep in the chair opposite me.

'Come on,' I said to Peter, 'Let me help you up to bed.'

'You go on,' he replied. 'I'll join you in a second. I just need to help myself to some coffee.'

I ran quietly up the stairs, checked on Tina, brushed my teeth, threw myself down and fell asleep.

The following day was my day off. By the time I awoke Peter had already gone to work. I went downstairs to find Kate in the kitchen. 'I don't know how he does it,' I said as I approached her. She looked up, noticed that Peter's bag was gone from the top of the cupboard and smiled.

'Where's Tina?' I asked.

'At your Mum's,' she replied. I wandered off towards the front room, where I found Robert still asleep. Something gave way inside me as I shouted, 'Get out!' Slowly he opened his eyes. 'Get out now before I throw you out!' I continued to scream, as I threw his shoes frantically at him.

'You fucking bitch!' he snapped at me as he tried to put his shoes on. 'Wait until Peter hears about this.'

'Do I look bothered?' I retorted. I grabbed him and dragged him towards the door. 'Just get out!'

I pushed him outside, threw his car keys behind him and then closed the door with a huge bang. 'Well done Natalie,' Kate said from behind me.

I watched from the window as Robert drove off, then I went across the road to collect Tina. I never took to Robert, who was an ambulance driver at the clinic where Peter worked. He lived somewhere in Kingstown, the capital, and would often drive to and from work when he was sober enough to do so. Other nights were spent on our settee. Although he could be pleasant enough, there was something about him that got right under my skin. He was just too bold and brassy.

I returned to find an angry Peter waiting for me. 'This is nice,' I said in vexation, as I approached him. 'You're waiting for me for a change.'

'How dare you!' he screamed. 'How dare you throw Robert out of my house!'

With Tina and Kate looking on, Peter and I argued continuously. Mum, who heard the shouting from across the street, entered the house and bellowed, 'What the hell is going on here?' All heads turned in her direction. Kate took Tina, who was now in tears, right outside the house. 'Oh Mum!' I cried as I found comfort in her arms once again.

'Look at you,' Peter bellowed. 'You're a right little mummy's girl, aren't you?'

We started arguing again. Mum left the room, in quite a hurry. I broke into tears. 'Go on, cry!' Peter shouted. I ran out, and up the stairs towards the bedroom. 'Go on, run to Mummy,' he shouted from behind.

I listened in fright as he tore the room apart with his fists and legs. 'Come on Natalie,' Mum said as she joined me. 'You and Tina are coming home with me.' She went towards the wardrobe and started to gather my things.

'Leave it, Mum,' I screamed, 'please.' Astonished at the tone of my voice, she turned towards me. My tears were uncontrollable.

'I'm sorry, Mum,' I cried, 'but I have to sort this one out for myself.'

The front door slammed, and I ran to the window. I watched as Peter jumped into his car and then disappeared down the road. 'I wish he would tell me what's troubling him,' I said, turning to Mum, as she began mopping my tears.

'I hate to see you like this,' she replied.

'Mummy, Mummy!' Tina shouted as she ran towards me and straight onto my lap. I closed my eyes, held her tight and thought hard of the one person I longed for: Tommy.

Mum stayed until we were settled and then she left, with Tina. Half an hour later Peter returned. Ashamed, he hung his head low and whispered 'Hi.' Slowly I turned away and replied, 'Hello, Peter.' There was complete silence for a short while. Together we both tried to apologise, then together we laughed.

'Come here,' I said, beckoning him as he tried to take off his shoes. I took him into my arms and listened as he sobbed on my shoulder.

'I'm sorry Natalie,' he cried. 'I'm so sorry.'

'Whatever is the matter, Peter?' I asked softly. 'Let's talk about it. There was a time when we used to talk about everything.'

He broke away and leaned forward. I watched as he clasped his hands over his face, uttering something I didn't understand. He looked at me, forced a smile, kissed me gently, apologised again, and then walked off.

Quickly I followed in his footsteps. 'Come on, Peter,'

I said from behind him. 'Talk to me, please tell me what it is that is troubling you.' He stood still as I caught up with him and he turned towards me. 'Is it the wedding?' I asked.

'Yes,' he answered, to my surprise. He began to explain how frightened he was of making the same mistake again. I wanted to believe him but I couldn't, for deep down I knew that he was not telling me the truth. Something was troubling Peter, and it definitely was not our upcoming wedding.

The household gradually returned to normal. Peter became my Peter again. Robert still called round to see him, but only when I was out, for he was trying his best to avoid me and I him.

The wedding was now three months away and preparations were in full swing. Kate and Mum seemed to be more excited than I was. I still hadn't got to the root of Peter's problem though.

One morning over breakfast he took hold of my hand and looked deep into my eyes. My body shivered at his touch, for his hands were as cold as ice. His eyes were sad and he seemed somewhat confused.

'What is it darling?' I asked, clasping my hands over his in an effort to provide warmth. His lips parted, and then closed again.

'What is it, Peter?' I said again. He smiled and said, 'Nothing. I just wanted to tell you how much I love you.' He broke away, and we ate breakfast in silence.

That day was his day off and as I kissed him goodbye at the front door, I squeezed his hands gently and said, 'Please talk to me, Peter.'

'Off to work,' he replied. 'You'll be late.'

As I drove to work Peter's image lingered on my mind for the entire journey. At work I found it impossible to concentrate, for I was deep in thought. Whatever was troubling him? I asked myself that over and over again. If only he would talk to me. It was unbearable.

I couldn't go through another day not knowing what the problem was, so I jumped into my car and headed for home. It was twelve thirty; Tina would be at school and Kate would be out shopping. I smiled at this thought, for I knew that Peter and I would have the house to ourselves.

As I drove up I noticed that Robert's car was parked on our driveway behind Peter's. I reversed and parked across the street. I turned the key in the lock and walked into the house. It was quiet. I looked in the kitchen, then in the front room, but they were nowhere to be seen. Maybe they were in the garden. I closed the study door.

Then suddenly I heard Peter's laughter coming from upstairs. 'Finally he's got round to changing that faulty light switch,' I said to myself as I ran hurriedly up the stairs and arrived at our bedroom door.

I turned the handle and flung the door open. I stood in the doorway in stunned silence, staring bewildered and astounded. Peter and Robert were lying there together in our bed. They turned towards me in complete shock. Their naked bodies sent shock waves through my body, and I threw up my breakfast all over the carpet.

I ran with trembling hands and knees down the stairs. 'Natalie, Natalie!' Peter called after me repeatedly. I threw the front door open and sent Kate and her shopping flying to the ground. I did not look back as she cried out in agony. I skipped angrily over the scattered groceries, jumped over Kate and ran head first towards the old shed. I arrived at the shed shaking like a leaf.

'This is a dream,' I cried loudly pinching myself. 'This must be a dream.' Then Peter entered the barn. Topless and shoeless, he stood at the doorway looking at me.

'Tell me I'm dreaming, Peter!' I cried out. 'Please tell me it's all a dream!'

'Natalie,' he said, advancing towards me, 'I'm so sorry.'

'Believe me, the last thing I wanted to do was to hurt you,' he protested.

It wasn't a dream; it was all horribly real. I exploded in anger. 'Fuck you, Peter Rhodes!' I cried. 'Fuck you!'

He put out his hand in an effort to take hold of me. 'Don't touch me!' I screamed. 'Don't you fucking touch me!'

'Natalie, please,' he said softly, still advancing towards me. I picked up a log that was lying on the floor nearby and lashed out at him with all my might. 'You fucking bastard!' I screamed as I hit him repeatedly. He fell to the floor and I continued beating him with a fury over which I had no control. Someone grabbed me from behind and I fought hard to break free. 'Natalie, stop!' Kate's voice echoed. I dropped the blood-covered log, as I turned around to face her.

Some of the villagers entered the shed and a few seconds later someone shouted, 'Please call an ambulance'. I was still shaken as Kate led me around Peter's still form and away from the shed. 'You fucking asshole!' I screamed at him, lashing out with a final kick.

Kate grabbed me. 'Enough, Natalie, that's enough,' she shouted.

By this time the street was crowded with inquisitive villagers. 'What the fuck are you all looking at?' I screamed. I broke loose of Kate's hold on me and forced my way through the crowd. The villagers looked at me in shock, for never before had they heard such language escape my lips.

When I arrived home, Kate tucked me comfortably into bed like a baby. I awoke about two hours later and found Mum sitting quietly beside me. I could tell by her swollen eyes that she had been crying.

'Hello, dear,' she said, taking hold of my hand as I sat upright. She held me tightly in her arms. 'Now are you going to tell me what happened?'

I took a deep breath and replied, 'No I don't want to talk about it.'

'Is it another woman?' she asked.

Breaking away from her embrace, I shouted, 'Mum, I'm sorry but I just don't want to talk about it.'

Before she could reply, there was a loud knocking at the door. Kate arrived, looking very upset.

'What is it, Kate?' Mum asked. Kate seemed speechless.

'Kate, I bellowed, 'what is it?'

'Natalie,' she replied, 'the police... they are downstairs waiting to see you.'

'Oh my god!' Mum gasped. I was petrified and fought hard to swallow the large lump I had suddenly developed in my throat. Since the ambulance had taken Peter off to the hospital, we knew nothing of his condition.

I took a deep breath and walked carefully down the stairs to join the two police officers who were waiting for me. As Mum and I approached, the two officers rose, advanced towards us and introduced themselves. Mum sat quietly by my side as they filled us in on Peter's condition. We learnt that he was still in hospital, was badly shaken up and had a broken arm.

They asked me over and over again to explain in every detail the events of the entire day and what had happened in the shed. I pleaded innocence. I lied that I had gone to the shed and found Peter lying there. I knew the villagers would back me, for to them Peter Rhodes was still an outsider.

The police officers left, as they couldn't do anything until they heard Peter's side of the story. Before they left they clearly indicated that I would be hearing from them again.

I felt no sympathy at all for Peter and was so angry with him that I even wished he would die. I looked out of the window and realised that the street was deserted. The excitement was now over, and everyone had gone home.

It was then that I saw Robert's black BMW still parked in the drive behind Peter's Volvo. This sent streams of renewed anger down my spine. I picked up a cutlass. My mind seemed to explode as I threw the front door open and ran shoeless, cutlass in hand, towards the drive.

At the front of the house I angrily smashed the headlights of Robert's car. I was so angry that I did not notice the blood gushing from my hand.

'Natalie, Natalie!' Mum's voice echoed over the noise of all the breaking glass. I stood still, shaking with anger. 'Come on, dear,' she said, comforting me once again. 'Come inside,' she said, leading the way. Sweat poured from my body like a kettle boiling over.

Mum put me safely in the kitchen and Kate made me a much-needed strong drink. I took hold of the glass and instantly felt nauseous again as I remembered the events of the day and what I had seen earlier. I threw the glass to the floor and shouted, 'Come on, Kate, pack my stuff. I'm going home.'

Mum came into the kitchen and looked at the stained floor. 'Are you sure about this, moving out I mean?' she asked.

'Yes Mum,' I replied, as I ran hurriedly up the stairs. 'Come on, give me a hand.'

'Only you could attack a car with a cutlass,' she joked.

We spent most of the evening moving all of Tina's and

my belongings back to Mum's place. Kate phoned her husband and he kindly came along with two of his brothers to help. Everyone avoided talking about the day's events. We were so busy that we didn't even notice the time.

'That's the last of your things,' Mum said, as we finally came downstairs.

'I'm completely worn out,' said Kate. I smiled at them both and said thank you. Then the tears returned. 'Come on,' Mum said, 'let me make us all something to eat.'

'Sounds like a brilliant idea to me,' Kate replied.

'You two go on' I said, still in tears, 'I'll be over soon.'

'Are you sure?' asked Mum.

'Yes, don't worry. I'll only be a minute.'

They left the house and I listened as they closed the door behind them. I stayed where I was and listened as they made their way down the outside steps. In a daze I slowly walked around the house room after room, remembering the good times and the bad times. I threw myself down at the bottom of the stairs and cried, wishing that the wind would take the sound of my voice across the sea, straight into the depths of Tommy's heart.

CHAPTER 9

THE VISIT

Tina and I settled back at home, and in a few weeks it was as if we had never left. I heard nothing about Peter and I made no effort to find out his whereabouts. Mum wasn't happy that I was refusing to see him. I told her nothing about what had led up to Peter being hospitalised and rumours of all sorts were floating around the village, but no one other than Kate and I actually knew the truth.

One evening as I was going in through the front door, Kate came bursting out on her way home. We crashed into each other. 'Sorry,' we both apologised. 'Bye,' said Kate as she ran down the stairs. I watched as she swung her bag to and fro, whistling softly.

'Kate!' I shouted, before she crossed the road. She halted, turned around and smiled at me. 'Can I have a word?' I asked.

'Sure you can,' she replied. I caught up with her and took a deep breath. 'Kate,' I muttered, fighting hard to bring out the words. She stared expectantly at me. 'Kate.' I continued nervously, but again words failed me. She took hold of my hand and said, 'I didn't see anything.'

I was still speechless, and suddenly I felt ashamed. I blushed with embarrassment.

'Stop worrying, Natalie,' she said, and with that she was gone. I watched as she disappeared around the corner. 'Mummy, Mummy!' an excited Tina shouted from the porch. 'Hello, my darling,' I replied. I ran towards her and scooped her up.

The next day I received a letter from Betty, who was coming to visit for the weekend. This really cheered me up, for it would be great to see her again. When I told her about Peter and the separation on the phone, she was very concerned and was sorry that she wasn't there for me to lend support. Before I left for work, I asked Kate to prepare the spare room for her as she was arriving the following day.

'Auntie Betty is coming to see you tomorrow,' I said to Tina. She looked at me and smiled as if she really understood, even though the last time Betty had seen her she'd been only a few months old.

Betty arrived on the Friday night and I picked her up from the station. She was exactly the same - tall, beautiful and happy. On the way home we stopped at the village café and there I poured my heart out to her. I filled her in on everything. I told her what I had seen that morning and about Peter being hospitalised.

'The dirty swine!' she blurted out loudly. Customers in the café turned and stared at us. 'Oh Natalie, darling,' she sympathised taking hold of my hand. 'You poor sweet thing, I'm ever so sorry. Come,' she said softly. 'Let me take you home, I'll drive.'

On the way home she filled me in on what had been happening. Her business was rapidly expanding, and she now owned two more shops. Her brother had just got engaged and most of all, she was healthy and very happy, and I was pleased for her.

As she was driving up the driveway, I noticed that she was wearing a diamond engagement ring similar to the one Peter had given me. As the car halted, I took hold of her hand and said, 'Betty, this is beautiful - really beautiful.'

'Thank you,' she replied with a gentle smile.

'Why didn't you tell me?' I asked.

'Bad timing,' she replied.

'Congratulations,' I said as I held her close.' 'Now come inside, we must celebrate. I want to know every little detail.'

'OK', she replied. 'Have you got all night?' Together we laughed, collected the bags and went indoors.

Betty's laughter brought the house back to life. She joined Tina playing various games, while I listened from the kitchen, where I was busy helping to prepare the meal.

Kate turned to me and said, 'You're lucky to have such a wonderful friend.'

'I know,' I replied.

Later Betty took the liberty of reading Tina a bedtime story and tucking her up. Kate left, then we sat down to supper and she filled us in on her new-found love. His name was Dennis Smith. He was unemployed and eighteen years her senior. He had been married twice and had five children from previous marriages.

Suddenly she paused and looked at our puzzled faces. We were lost for words. 'I know what you two are thinking,' she said, full of excitement. 'My entire family hates him, but what the hell, I love him, he makes me so happy. You two have got to meet him, he is such a wonderful man.'

'If you love Dennis and he loves you, then marry him you must,' said Mum. 'You can't let anything or anyone stand in the way of true love.'

'Thank you Mrs Steinford,' she replied, smiling broadly. I turned away sharply, for I did not dare to meet her eyes. Deep down I felt that Betty's lifetime of happiness was about to come to an end. But who was I to judge? Unlike Mum, I decided to keep my opinion to myself until I met Dennis. Betty was my best friend and I wanted nothing but the best for her.

'Natalie,' someone interrupted, as my thoughts drifted. I looked up and was confronted by two smiling faces.

'Are you all right?' asked Betty.

'Yes,' I replied with a forced smile. 'Congratulations

darling.' Our glasses touched and together Mum and I chorused 'To Dennis and Betty.'

That night Betty and I sat in my room and we talked about Dennis.

'Are you sure you're doing the right thing? I asked.

'Yes,' she replied. 'It just feels right.'

I smiled and though still not convinced, I held her tight and once again expressed my congratulations. I would rest more easily after meeting Dennis at the engagement party in three weeks' time. That night we sat up talking for hours. It was about midday the next day when Kate and Tina found us asleep on my bedroom floor.

It was Saturday, my day off. 'What are your plans for today?' asked Betty.

'I thought you and I could take Tina shopping,' I replied. 'I've got to buy her a few things.'

'That sounds like fun,' she said, as she tickled an excited Tina.

Two hours later we were dressed and ready for our shopping spree. As I was about to open the front door there was a loud knock. I opened it to be confronted by an elderly man, about ten years Mum's senior, smartly dressed and pleasant. Tall and slim, he stood staring at me, with the most comforting warm smile. Had he lost his way?

'Can I help you?' I asked. He made no reply but continued his stare. 'Sir,' I repeated, 'can I help you?' Still no reply. I tapped him gently on his shoulder and with that, he replied, 'Please forgive me young lady, I think I might have the wrong house.' With that he turned speedily around, jumped into a green Land Rover which was parked in front of my car, then drove off slowly.

'How weird,' Betty said from behind me.

'Indeed,' I replied. We said goodbye to Kate and were on our way.

We spent the afternoon shopping, and Tina was enjoying every minute. She ran around happily with Betty, who loved spoiling her rotten. At the end of the day, Tina was completely shattered and fell asleep on the back seat on the way home. Was she, I wondered, somewhere over that famous rainbow?

As we approached home, I noticed Mrs Rhodes coming down Peter's steps, carrying a few bags. She looked up, saw me and stood still. Betty followed my gaze. Quickly I parked the car, finding it impossible to swallow as huge lumps of fear gathered in my throat. I still knew nothing of Peter's condition, nor had I had any more visits from the police. Tina was still asleep on the back seat. With shaking hands and knees I managed to leave the car and closed the door quietly behind me. Betty did likewise.

Mrs Rhodes and I looked at each other from across the street in complete silence. Then suddenly she ran towards her car and jumped in. 'Mrs Rhodes!' I called, as I ran across the road, trying to catch her before she drove off. I was in such a hurry that I did not see Betty as she chased after me. Mrs Rhodes turned the key, but the car refused to start.

'Mrs Rhodes, can I have a word? Mrs Rhodes, please!' I cried, as I banged on the car window. She turned and looked at me furiously, eyes wild with anger. Her window came down a few inches and she threw a small box toward me, and shouted, 'Peter wants you to keep this.'

I collected the box and opened it. It was the engagement ring Peter had given to me. I was speechless. Seeing my reaction, she jumped from the car and threw me to the ground. 'I hope you rot in hell, Natalie Steinford!' she screamed, throwing punches at me. 'Rot in hell!'

I covered my face as best I could, and shouted, 'Get her off me somebody please!' Betty pulled her loose, and she burst into tears. Panting for breath, she managed to say, 'You've let me down Natalie, I had my doubts, but I believed in you. I really did.'

'Mrs Rhodes, please hear me out!' I cried. With that she jumped back into her car, spat at me through the window and sped off. My body ached. Betty helped me up and gently wiped my bleeding upper lip. 'I can't believe this,' I stammered. 'The bastard hasn't told her the truth, has he?'

'No, he has not,' replied Betty as she led me safely home. I turned around, and noticed that the neighbours were once again putting their curtains back into place, for the show was once again over.

I took a much-needed bath, as I was covered in dirt and dust. As I was getting dressed, I heard Mum call. 'Come in,' I said. Mum appeared, looking very concerned.

'Are you OK?' she asked. 'Kate told me what happened.'

'I'm fine Mum,' I replied, not looking at her. As she got closer, I looked up, and she said. 'Your lips need seeing to, I'll fetch the antiseptic ointment.'

'Don't worry Mum, I've already done it, I just need some time on my own.'

'OK, I'll see you later, get some rest.' With that she was gone.

I went downstairs about three hours later to find Kate in the kitchen. 'Where is Tina?' I asked.

'Asleep,' she replied.

'Mum and Betty?'

'They went out about an hour ago, they haven't returned yet.'

'Thanks Kate, I'll be in the study if you need me.'

I went to the study, opened a book and sat in the comfortable armchair. My mind drifted as I remembered the events of the day. What had started out as a perfectly wonderful day had ended so nastily. I felt sad and was in a tearful state, to say the least.

Mum and Betty returned, and I tried hard to wipe away the tears. Betty handed me some tissues and said 'You look as though you need these.' Kate then brought us three glasses of freshly-made guava juice. As she left, I asked, 'Where did you two disappear to?' Their expressions changed. 'What's wrong?' I asked. No one replied. 'Come on, talk to me,' I continued.

'We went to see Peter.'

'You did what?' I bellowed, looking at them both

with disappointment. There was utter silence. 'You had no right!' I screamed.

'Natalie...' began Betty.

'How is he?' I surprised myself by asking.

'He's fine, he asked after you and Tina. I think he's planning on coming back to Dickson soon.'

'I can't be living across the road from that man!' I screamed. 'I don't ever want to see him again.'

Mum was very quiet. 'What is it, Mum?' I asked.

'It just hurts so much, when I think about all that you've been through.'

I looked at Betty and my suspicions were confirmed. She had told Mum. I had trusted her. 'You told her!' I screamed. 'Why, Betty? I trusted you!'

I was angry and ashamed, so ashamed I couldn't even look at Mum. 'I'm sorry Natalie,' Betty cried. 'Mrs Rhodes was at home, she was still very upset, accusing you of all sorts.'

'You told Mrs Rhodes?'

'Yes. She kept on and on calling you every name under the sun, so I had to.'

'Thanks a million, Betty!' I screamed, as I headed out. 'It's really nice to know that I have such a loyal and trusting friend.'

'Natalie, Natalie, I'm sorry, I'm so sorry.'

I did not look back. I ran to the old shed and threw myself down. I didn't know what to do. If only Tommy had been there. Suddenly I found myself on my knees and about to pray, something I did on a regular basis, especially when I was in trouble or in real need. I took a deep, deep breath, closed my eyes and slowly poured my heart out to God.

'That was beautiful,' a familiar voice whispered, from behind me. I turned to look at Mum. 'How long have you been standing there?' I asked.

'Long enough.' She helped me to rise. 'Now tell me, what was that all about earlier on?'

'Sorry Mum, I didn't want you to know.'

'But I thought we talked about everything?'

'We do,' I whispered, 'but I found it so embarrassing.'

She held me close and rested my head gently upon her breast. 'Never mind dear, at least you found out before it was too late.'

'I haven't got a problem with his sexuality Mum, it just hurts because of the way I found out. How could he not tell me? I knew something was troubling him. Why did he not tell me? I really adored him. How did Mrs Rhodes take the news?'

'She didn't believe a word, she called Betty a liar.'

'Poor woman,' I muttered, as we hugged and walked towards the house. 'By the way mum, a gentleman called round earlier,' I said, suddenly remembering the stranger.

'A gentleman!' she chuckled. 'It's been a long time since I've had one of those knocking on my door. What did he want?'

'Nothing, he said he had come to the wrong house.'

'That's a shame,' she said, as we entered the house in laughter. I looked at her aged face and sighed happily, for I found Mum so comforting. I couldn't remember when she hadn't been there for me. No matter what the situation, she always found a way of cheering her little girl up, and for that I shall love her always.

I awoke the following day and decided it was time to visit Peter - I felt strong and brave. I discussed my plans with the rest of the household.

'Are you nervous?' Betty asked.

'No,' I replied confidently.

'Would you like me to accompany you?'

'No thanks, this is something I have to do on my own,' I said with a smile.

'OK then, if you're sure.'

'I'm positive. Now how do I look?' I turned around slowly.

'Gorgeous as always,' Mum replied as she joined us.

'Thanks Mum. Where are you going?' I had noticed that she was dressed, handbag in hand. 'It's Sunday, you're not going to work are you?'

'No,' she replied.

'Well, why are you dressed, where are you going?' Betty interrupted.

'I'm going with Natalie.'

'Mum, you don't have to, I'd rather go on my own.'

'No,' she insisted, 'I'm going with you.'

I have never ever beaten Mum in an argument, so I gave in. Half an hour later we were on our way, Mum looking snug in the driver's seat.

Some forty minutes later we arrived at Belle View, a small mountainous village also on the windward side of the Island. As we parked outside Mrs Rhodes' sky blue three-bedroom bungalow, I asked Mum to wait in the car. I took a deep breath, and went on confidently through the huge gate. Then I banged loudly on the door.

A pleasantly-dressed Mrs Rhodes appeared seconds later. Astonished, she stood looking at me. Neither of us spoke as she stepped aside, allowing me inside. I walked in and headed straight for Peter's room, the room he had occupied from birth, which he always escaped to from time to time. I knew he'd be sitting in bed feeling sorry for himself.

I opened the door and he looked up and saw me. 'What happened to your lip?' he asked, concerned.

'I tripped and fell,' I lied. The room was completely silent. 'So how are you?' I asked, trying hard to appear normal.

'I'm fine, thank you,' he replied. A strained silence followed. Peter looked at the window like a lost soul. 'Natalie, I'm so sorry for what happened,' he finally said. 'I know you will not find it easy to forgive me, but believe me when I say that I tried to tell you, I really did. I finally told Mum this morning.'

'Why did you wait so long to tell her?' I asked.

'I tried telling her years ago, but it was difficult. The timing was never right, I knew it would tear her apart, she's so religious and has her strong Catholic beliefs.'

'Just give her some time, she'll come around, she loves you very much, and no matter what, she will always love you.'

'I'm sorry you found out the way you did, Natalie,' he said. 'I do love you, you know that don't you?'

'Stop it Peter,' I cried, 'please stop it.' He sat upright and beckoned to me. 'No Peter,' I said sternly, 'we both know you will never be completely satisfied with me, I've got Tina to consider. You treated us so well, and for that we will always be eternally grateful, but you must follow your heart. Grab happiness when it's offered to you, Peter. I'm sorry I reacted the way I did. I didn't mean to hurt you.'

'I know,' he replied. With that I rushed towards him and hugged him with all my might. As we broke loose, I kissed him gently.

'I'll see you around,' I said, as I headed for the door. I paused at the doorway, turned, and said, 'Goodbye Peter, and good luck.' I closed the door behind me and walked off briskly.

'Natalie, Natalie!' He called from behind me. I did not look back.

CHAPTER 10

THE STRANGER

On the way home we stopped at the village shop to buy a few special things for supper, as a treat for Betty. It was her last day with us. I waited in the car while Mum went in. I turned around wearily, and saw the stranger who had come to our house the day before. There he was, walking hurriedly past the car, then into the shop. He turned around, looked at me, managed a smile and a wave, then went inside. I returned both his smile and his wave. 'What a strange man,' I remember thinking.

Exhausted, I fell asleep. I was awoken by someone tooting their horn. I looked at my watch and realised I had been in the car for over an hour. Where was Mum,

I wondered, as I locked the car and headed into the shop.

'Hello Mabel!' I shouted to the assistant. 'Have you seen Mum?'

'She's out the back,' she replied.

'What is she doing out there? It's her day off, she's not meant to be working.'

'I'll fetch her for you, Natalie.'

I watched as she disappeared, then reappeared again, looking confused, a few seconds later. 'She'll be out in a minute,' she managed.

Just then, the elderly stranger I had seen entering the shop rushed past Mabel, bumping into me in the process. He paused, apologised, then was on his way like the bullet from a gun.

'That man is always in a hurry,' I said to Mabel. 'Who is he, anyway?'

Before she could reply, Mum re-entered the shop from the back. Her face was flushed, her eyes puffed and swollen, and she appeared very nervous.

'Mum, are you all right, what's wrong?' I asked.

'I'm fine, Natalie dear,' she replied, 'I'm just very tired.' I knew her only too well. Something or someone had upset her, and she didn't want me to know. Confused, I watched as she tried to collect the groceries needed for supper. As she walked over to the wine section I turned to look at Mabel. A few seconds later there was a huge crash, as bottles of wine hit the floor. Mabel and I ran immediately to her aid.

Mum was in tears and shaking like a leaf. 'I'm

sorry,' she cried. She was trying to pick up broken pieces of glass, cutting her hand in the process.

'Mum!' I shouted, 'whatever is the matter?' I helped her to her feet. She made no reply.

'Natalie, you take her home, and I'll clean this up.' said Mabel.

'Thanks Mabel.' I led Mum to the car. 'What's wrong Mum?' I asked again.

'I don't know what came over me dear, you know how emotional I get sometimes.'

'But Mum...'

'Don't worry Natalie, I'm OK.' She smiled. 'Everything is OK, trust me.'

I opened the car door and watched in silence as she sat down and fumbled with her seat belt. I had never seen her like this. I knew that something had happened in the shop. Whether it had something to do with the stranger or something else, I didn't know. All I knew was that something had deeply upset my mother, and whatever it was I had to find out.

We arrived home, and soon it was as if the episode at the shop had never happened. Mum kept busy around the house doing her usual chores. Seeing her back to normal convinced me that she was indeed OK, and the matter was soon forgotten. If it was all an act, she was a very good actress.

Betty returned home and everything went back to normal. The weeks dragged slowly on and still there was no sign of life over at Peter's house. 'He must be back to work by now,' I told myself on several occasions.

I couldn't wait to visit Betty in New Montrose for her engagement party. We were only going for the weekend, but I felt relieved knowing that I was going to be away from Dickson Village, something I didn't do very often.

Then as I was rounding the bend leading toward my home one evening on my return from work, a familiar green Land Rover came swerving round the corner in front of me. It was Dickson's new addition - the stranger I had last seen rushing from the village shop.

I turned my car around and followed him and blew my horn in a desperate attempt to attract his attention. He must have seen me, but he made no effort to stop. Instead he increased his speed in an effort to lose me, but I did likewise and kept on his tail.

As we approached a pedestrian crossing, he took no notice and rushed through at full speed. Angry drivers in both directions blew their horns furiously. I slammed on my brakes and came to a safe halt as startled pedestrians appeared in front of me. Angrily I watched as the Land Rover disappeared into the distance.

The weeks dragged on and finally it was time for our weekend away. I was overcome with happiness. We were now packed and on our way to New Montrose in Kingstown. Kate decided to accompany us at the last minute and sat quietly with Tina in the back seat. All the years I had known Betty, I had never been to her home town. I was extremely happy that I was finally on my way.

After driving through the crowded capital busy with the hustle and bustle of my country people, we arrived at Lewis Street some two hours later. 'Wow, how beautiful!' remarked Kate. We drove slowly through the large electric gates, admiring the spectacular surroundings. As the car halted, Betty ran towards us from the house in excitement. I jumped from the wheel, ran straight towards her, and we hugged longingly.

'Well,' she said, 'you're in New Montrose at long last. Welcome.'

'Thank you,' I said with a smile as she turned to greet Mum and Kate. Taking hold of Tina, she shouted, 'Come on, come inside, the others are waiting.'

'What about our bags?' Kate asked.

'Don't worry about the bags, Anthony will fetch them later.'

We went into the house and cheerfully greeted everyone. We knew everyone except Suzette, Anthony's fiancée. Suzette was absolutely charming and adorable. Her short black hair lay lazily above her shoulders and her ebony skin shone brightly with sheer radiance. She was about five foot two. She greeted us with warmth.

'Where is Dennis?' I asked Betty.

'He'll be along later, he'll be joining us for supper.'

'I can't wait to meet him,' I said, taking hold of her hand. 'I'm very happy for you.'

'Thanks Natalie,' she replied with a smile.

We were then shown to our rooms. Exhausted, I

collapsed on the beautifully-made four-poster mahogany bed.

Two hours later, we arrived downstairs for supper washed, dressed and feeling fully refreshed. As I entered the dining room a slender, well-dressed gentleman stood up with arms extended to greet me. Noticing this, Betty joined him. Puzzled, I looked at Betty, her brown eyes dazzled with excitement.

'Natalie this is Dennis, Dennis this is Natalie,' she said with pride, as he took my hand in his. I was spellbound, for Dennis was nothing like the local I had expected him to be.

'Hello Natalie,' he said, breaking my trance, 'it is wonderful to meet you at last, I've heard so much about you.'

'All good, I hope,' I managed to joke. 'It's a pleasure to meet you Dennis.'

As we all sat down I glanced around the table. There was a mixture of faces, some blank, others puzzled and confused, but one face shone brightly above the rest - Betty's, glowing with pure excitement. That was all the convincing I needed.

Supper was eaten in silence, for Dennis's presence seemed to make Betty's family uneasy. I was extremely happy when the meal was over and we adjourned to the huge front room. Dennis sat opposite Betty; he seemed restless, yet very proud. Betty was still oozing with excitement. They looked at each other longingly and lovingly. They were truly in love.

The wedding was two months away, and as Anthony and Suzette were also getting married they had decided to make it a double wedding. I couldn't wait, for I always enjoyed weddings and was very proud when Betty asked me to be her maid of honour. Tina fell asleep, and I excused myself and took her upstairs to bed. I knew that Betty was going to follow me.

A few seconds later we were sitting side by side looking down at a peaceful Tina.

'Tell me, what do you think of Dennis? Betty said, after a while.

'Well, to be honest, he is not at all what I was expecting. Where's he from anyway?'

She made no reply.

'I'm sorry, probably I'm being a bit too harsh.'

'That's all right,' she said. 'I love him so much, Natalie.'

'I know you do darling, and he loves you too, it's so obvious.'

'If only my family would see that, and accept my wishes,' she said.

'They'll come round in good time dear, stop worrying.' I replied.

'There's something else I want to tell you Natalie. I'm pregnant.'

'Oh Betty, that's great news, have you told the rest of the family?'

'No, I wanted to tell you all at supper. The timing wasn't right, but I will soon.'

We talked for a while, then re-joined the party downstairs.

'Where's Kate?' I asked.

'Where she always is, in the kitchen,' replied Mum. The room filled with laughter as Kate appeared carrying a tray of refreshments. 'I heard that, Mrs Steinford,' she laughed.

Dennis gestured for me to follow him as he made his way toward the porch. I blinked at Betty, then followed him. Together we sat down.

'Abandoning the crew are you?' I said.

'I don't think I would be greatly missed,' he replied.

'Give them time.'

We talked and talked for quite some time. The more I spoke to him, the more I got to know and, surprisingly, like him. He was filled with joy and was so proud of Betty and their unborn child. He confirmed that he had had two previous failed marriages and had five children, who also adored Betty. He said he was a crazy American who had visited the country on holiday, met his first wife, fallen in love, married her and settled in Layou, a village about twelve miles away on the leeward side of Kingstown.

Together we chatted as though we were long-lost friends. We lost track of time.

'I've been looking for you two everywhere,' said Betty as she joined us.

'Now you've found us young lady, what can we do for you?' Dennis teased, inviting her forward. She sat gently on his lap. As he wrapped his arms around her, smoothly their lips touched.

'Now, if you two would excuse me, it's time I retired to bed,' I said.

'No you don't have to,' Betty replied.

'Yes I do, it's been a long day and I'm very tired darling.'

'OK. After all, I need you alert and looking bright for a complete tour tomorrow.'

I said my goodnights, then exited, taking one final longing look at the lovers as they lost themselves in each other. I smiled a happy smile, for Betty had now found her Mr Right. They looked so good, so happy together.

The next day I arrived downstairs to find the house deserted. I heard a noise coming from the back garden, so I followed it. There I found Betty cleaning her walking boots.

'Good morning,' I said, as I kissed her. 'Where is everyone?'

'Anthony took them to Veejays rooftop restaurant and bar for breakfast, he wanted to wake you, but Mrs Steinford insisted that you had your rest.'

'That's Mum for you. Where's Dennis?'

'He left last night, you'll see him tomorrow at the party.'

'Is he not coming round tonight?'

'No he's not. I want to spend quality time with you as it's your first time here after countless invites. Now, are you ready for your tour? We'll grab something to eat on the way.'

'Sounds good to me, lead on.'

Kingstown was booming with early shoppers, and although it was early morning the sun was scorching hot. Music filled the air as traders gave shoppers samples of their CDs on sale. Pedestrians passed each other happily by. Everyone displayed such courtesy and warmth. It was as if everyone in the entire capital knew each other.

We walked lazily through the market where vendors sold their freshly picked organic produce - plantains, dasheen, okras, yam, eddoes, tania, plums, sugar cane, sugar apples, the list goes on and on. Everyone had their own stations. Some of the women wore big broad hats to keep the sun at bay while the men dressed simply in brightly-coloured string vest and shorts. Kingstown had so much to offer, so much to see and so much to do.

'Coconut water miss, one dollar?' a man politely asked, standing over a cart full of various coconuts, Spanish coconut and cutlass in hand at the ready.

'We'll take two,' Betty replied. We gulped the refreshing juice down and handed the empty nuts back to him.

'Would you like the jelly?' he asked, cutting both nuts in two.

'Yes please,' we chorused. We scooped the soft white jelly from the nuts with spoons made from the coconut's skin, looked at the man in satisfaction and headed on.

Street vendors lined the streets selling clothes, shoes, creams, soaps, breeze and many more products. We walked on past vans selling a wide variety of freshly-made coconut cakes and bread. On we walked past the huge post office and various banks. The scent of different varieties of local food from the nearby restaurants perfumed the air.

'Two snow cones please,' Betty asked a vendor as we entered Middle Street. I admired the shredded ice cone, drenched with a sweet cherry-flavoured juice and topped with condensed milk. We devoured our snow cones in what seemed like seconds. Betty took pleasure in showing me her shops in Middle Street. When we were done at the end of Middle Street we took a left and walked past the fire brigade, then another left turn past the Royal Police Force of St Vincent and the Grenadines, where a pleasant young smartly-dressed police officer stood in the entrance, gun in hand. On we went past Cobblestone, where the most expensive restaurants and hotels lie. I was exhausted as the sun was so hot.

There was a restaurant a few yards away just across the road from Y De Lima, one of the country's most famous stores, so we decided to pop in for a bite to eat. As we were about to enter the restaurant I glanced across the road and couldn't believe my eyes. I recognised the familiar green Land Rover which I had last seen speeding through Dickson Village. Instantly my energy was revived. My bags fell to the ground and I ran full speed ahead, pushing everyone out of my way and fighting my way through the crowds of busy shoppers.

'Natalie, Natalie!' Betty called from behind me, trying desperately to catch up. I did not turn around, for I was determined not to lose this stranger. I approached the Land Rover and banging with all my might on the closed window, I screamed, 'What do you want? Why are you following me?'

The driver looked up at me. I froze and my heart pounded when I saw his swollen eyes and tearful face. 'What do you want?' I said softly.

Betty finally caught up with me, carrying my bags, exhausted and gasping for breath. We didn't know what to say. Together we stood in silence, staring at the elderly man in the driver's seat.

'Why is he crying?' Betty asked quietly.

'How am I supposed to know?' I replied. 'What do you want with me?' I asked the stranger. He made no reply. 'Why are you following me?'

His wrinkled face creased. His lips parted in an attempt to speak, then closed again. He started the car engine. Betty and I stepped onto the pavement and watched as he drove slowly away. Further and further he drove, then he was gone.

'You've got to report him to the police,' said Betty.

'No, there's something about him that's intriguing me.'

'Natalie, this man has been following you, he's even been to your house, you've got to report him.'

Like my Mum, Betty always got the better of me, so the next two and a half hours was spent at the police station. With Betty's help I told them everything I knew about the stranger. An officer was assigned to follow us home and stay outside Betty's for my protection.

I was tired and hungry after the day's events. As we made our way back home I was restless, and thought hard about the stranger. Who was he? Whatever could he want with me?

As if reading my thoughts, Betty gently took my hand in hers and gave me a little squeeze. I smiled, and we drove home in silence with the officer on our tail.

As we parked the car, Mum came running out of the house. 'I was about to send a search party out for you two,' she said jokingly.

'Sorry Mum, but we have just spent two and a half hours at the police station,' I told her. She looked worried. 'The police station? Oh my god, what has happened?'

'Calm down Mum,' I replied, as I took her and led her inside. 'Everything is fine.'

Inside we told everyone about the day's events. 'I think you did the right thing,' Anthony said. Mum, who was now in tears, ran from the room. I ran after her. Finally I caught up with her at the back of the house, where she was crouching in a corner in floods of tears.

'Mum, what's wrong?' I asked. I knelt down beside her.

'I'm sorry Natalie, I'm so sorry!' she cried.

'What for? It's not your fault. Now come on, pull yourself together.' She looked at me with caring eyes, as if lost. 'Mum, what is it?'

She rose to her feet quickly, tidied herself and walked slowly into the house. 'Mum!' I called from behind her.

'Not now Natalie, goodnight.'

Baffled and confused, I watched as she walked on. Why did the mention of the stranger cause her so much pain? Were they old acquaintances? Whoever could he be?

'Natalie, are you all right out there?' Betty called through the window.

'Yes I'm fine, just coming, thank you,' I replied, as I headed back inside.

That night I found it impossible to sleep. I lay in bed twisting and turning, and I could tell from the sounds coming from Mum's room next door that she was doing the same.

I decided to get a drink from the kitchen, and noticed the lights were still on in Mum's room. I decided to pop my head in to see if she was OK. As I approached the door I heard voices coming from within, and recognised Betty's voice as she said 'Natalie has a right to know.'

A right to know what? I stood still and listened in silence as they continued.

'How can I tell her?' Mum replied. 'She's going to hate me - I know she will.'

'Natalie will never hate you, Mrs Steinford. She loves you, you were only trying to protect her.'

'But how can I tell her that her father is out of prison and wants to see her?'

My heart raced as the word 'father' echoed in my head. *Father? I haven't got a father. My father is dead.*

Mesmerised, I walked back to my room and lay down as images of the stranger in the green Land Rover flashed before me. I drifted back to the last time

I had seen him driving away. I remembered the sorrow, the pain and the loss I had seen in his eyes, the tears I had seen running down his face, the lines on his face as he had tried desperately to speak. Now I knew that the stranger who had followed me from Dickson Village to New Montrose was Percy Steinford, my father.

My head ached as thousands of questions raced through my mind. I tried to cry, but no tears came. Echoes of the word 'father' haunted me. Father, prison, my dad was in prison for some reason, what reason I knew not. I trembled at these thoughts. From childhood I had been made to believe that he had died in a car crash when I was a baby. This new development petrified me. I raced round the room, my head spinning in confusion. Sad and exhausted, I fell asleep some hours later.

CHAPTER 11

THE ENGAGEMENT PARTY

The next day was the day of Betty's engagement party. I awoke fully clothed, looked at the clock and noticed it was pretty late. I inspected myself in the mirror and realised that I looked disastrous. I felt exhausted and weak, for I had not had much sleep. I looked out the window in search of the police officer but he was nowhere to be seen.

I tried desperately to block out the conversation I had heard the previous night, for it was Betty's big day and I did not want to spoil it for her. Why couldn't anything go right for me? Once again my head began to ache as questions raced around inside.

There was a knock on the bathroom door. 'Just a minute, who is it?' I answered, as I wrapped a towel around me.

'It's Mum dear. I'm just going to take Tina for a walk and was wondering if you'd like to join us.'

My heart raced as I tried to reply, but I could not. 'Natalie, can you hear me?' she called. Still I couldn't reply; I stood glued to the spot. 'Natalie,' she called again. Then the handle turned and the door flew open.

I fought hard to avoid eye contact. 'Didn't you hear me calling you?' she asked. Suddenly the build-up of emotions I had been trying desperately to hide gave way. I pushed past her and ran from the bathroom, washing the carpets with my tears. I knew she was on my heel.

She followed me to the bedroom. I stood staring out of the window. 'Natalie dear, whatever is the matter?' she asked.

At that moment Betty appeared, and our heads turned in her direction. She sensed the situation. 'I'm sorry, I'll see you both downstairs,' she said.

'You know, don't you?' Mum asked as Betty left.

'Know what?' I replied angrily, as the tears continued to flow. She made no reply. 'Know what, Mum?' I shouted. 'Where is the police officer?'

Still she made no reply. We stood in complete silence for a while, my back turned, as I dared not look at her. I felt betrayed, hurt and angry. I could tell that she was now crying, but I did not care, my mother, my best friend, whom I trusted and loved had been lying to me all my life.

I turned as she started to move away. 'I'm ever so sorry,' she cried, 'really really sorry.' Before she could escape, I bellowed, 'Why didn't you tell me, Mum? Why have you been lying to me all these years? I was made to believe my father had died. Ha ha ha, I've got a dad! Tina has a granddad! Mum, you've got a hell of a lot of explaining to do. Why Mum, why?'

I looked up at her standing in the doorway, and felt nothing but hatred. I wanted answers, and I wanted them now. She looked at me, then left without saying another word. 'Mum!' I screamed after her, 'don't you walk away from me, I'm talking to you!' But she just continued walking off, and I banged the door behind her.

Mum had always held my hand and guided me through the pitfalls of life, but now I hated her. Was it sheer ungratefulness of the highest order to repay her with such hatred? What reason did she have to keep such a secret from me? Should I wait patiently until she was ready to talk to me? Who am I? Who really is Natalie Steinford?

I lay down and buried my head in the pillow, as countless questions took over.

Much later when I joined the party, it was in full swing. Betty met me at the bottom of the stairs. 'How are you doing?' she asked. 'I didn't want to disturb you, I thought you were better off left alone.'

'I'm OK, thanks.'

'Are you up to this?'

'Yes, I'll be fine,' I replied. I took a deep breath as she took my hand. I felt at ease as she took me around the room introducing me to her friends and other members of her family. My eyes searched desperately for my mother. Then just as I was about to ask Kate where she was, she came in to join us looking as beautiful as ever, dressed in a long white cotton maxi dress.

She stood still as our eyes met and smiled a very warm smile, and I managed a wave just before Anthony whisked her off to the dance floor. It was Betty's big night and I had to remain calm just for her.

Betty excused herself and went to join Dennis. With a glass of wine in hand I wandered around until finally I found myself sitting alone on the front porch. How long I stayed there I know not. My eyes drifted as I began counting the guest cars parked along the street, then suddenly I came to a halt. I recognised the third vehicle and its driver - my father.

Percy Steinford and I looked at each other, as he climbed out of the Land Rover and started walking towards me. I rose to my feet, brushing my clothes into shape nervously. We met at the bottom of the stairs, and the feeling I was experiencing was indescribable. For once I was truly lost for words.

'Hello Natalie,' he said softly, breaking the silence. I made no reply that I could remember. 'Natalie?' he repeated.

I forced a shy smile. 'I'm really sorry. All my life I have been made to believe that my father had died, and now you just pop up suddenly from nowhere.'

He looked at me with great pride, the tears again appearing in his eyes, but I stood strong.

'What exactly did your mum tell you?' he asked.

'I'm sorry, but I would appreciate it if you would leave us alone. Percy Steinford is not a part of our lives and that is the way it is going to stay. I'm very sorry, goodbye.' With that I about turned and headed hurriedly towards the house.

'Natalie please!' he cried, 'there isn't a day gone by when I haven't thought about my little girl. I love you, please give me five minutes!'

I halted and turned in his direction, 'I need time, I need to speak to Mum,' I said. 'I need explanations from her first.'

'I understand. Can I give you my address and phone number?'

'No, when I'm ready I'll find you. Goodbye.'

'Natalie!' he called as I continued to walk away. I breathed a deep sigh of relief. I was glad I had finally spoken to him. Why he had been in prison I did not know. I did not know why he was taking this sudden interest in me. Maybe the past was best left alone; we would see. For the moment I would let it rest until Mum was ready to talk to me about it.

CHAPTER 12

THE UNEXPECTED VISITOR

We returned to Dickson Village later the following day, and as we drove past Tommy's old house, I noticed that there was a 'FOR SALE' notice up outside. As I began to realise what this meant, I whispered to myself, 'welcome home Natalie'.

Gradually life got back to normal. We neither saw nor heard any more of Percy Steinford, and Mum still refused to talk about him. We learnt that Peter was now fully recovered and living with his mother temporarily. Two months later I bought Tommy's old house with the intention of renting it out, as I could not bring myself to live there again.

Tina continued to grow beautifully. The taller she grew, the more she looked like her dad. She enjoyed singing and dancing. She was truly my little treasure.

On my return from work one evening, I found the house deserted, and a note from Mum saying that they were in the village. The house was absolutely quiet, so I decided to take advantage of the opportunity by lying on the couch, television on, large glass of wine by my side. I must have dozed off for a few seconds when I was interrupted by a knock on the door. I ignored it, for I knew Mum and Kate had their key.

But the knock came again and again. 'Go away!' I hissed under my breath, but the person was very persistent. Finally I jumped to my feet and shouted, 'Just a second'. I finally reached the door and impatiently thrust it open, but there was no one to be seen. I looked up and down the street but there was not anyone in sight.

Puzzled, I returned inside and was about to close the door when a familiar deep, manly voice whispered softly, 'Hello Natalie.' I stood motionless, my heart thumping. Was I dreaming?

Then I heard that sweet voice again. 'Hello Natalie.'

'Tommy!' I screamed, 'Oh my god, Tommy!'

I turned to face the man standing before me, my long-lost love. He stood tall and strong looking down at me. Tears of joy flowed as he beckoned me to him. Without hesitation, I flung myself into his powerful embrace. His arms enveloped me with a caress I hoped would never end. I felt that wonderful feeling I had last felt when we had said our goodbyes at the airport years before, the sensation I had felt only for this one man. It overpowered me as our lips met.

'I've missed you so much,' he whispered.

'I've missed you too!' I cried.

Hand in hand, we entered the house. 'It is so wonderful to see you again, Tommy,' I said as we sat side by side on the couch. 'You look great.'

Gently he caressed me. 'Thank you,' he replied, 'you haven't changed a bit.' He flicked my hair into place.

We spent the next few hours telling each other all that had been happening since we last met. He was now a qualified doctor. I listened in silence as he proudly entertained me with his English lifestyle; he was clearly so happy. I knew I had to tell him about Tina, for they were due back home at any moment, but I thought it would be rude of me to interrupt - after all we had not seen each other in years.

'Natalie, I'm so sorry,' he whispered, catching my distant gaze. 'Here I am rabbiting on and on. I didn't mean to bore you.'

'No go on, I love listening to you,' I said. 'How long are you back for?'

'Two weeks.'

'Two weeks? Tommy, we haven't seen each other in years, and you're telling me that you'll be gone again in two weeks? It's crazy!'

'But I've got to go back to work.'

'Why did you bother coming back?' I let go of his hand and angrily walked towards the kitchen.

'I came back to get you,' he replied.

I stopped in my tracks. 'What did you say?' I asked, turning slowly in his direction.

'I came to get you, Natalie,' he repeated. My life is empty without you. I miss you so much. There has been no one else but you. You never replied to any of my letters, you never took any of my calls. I thought I had lost you. Here I am Natalie, standing in front of you in an effort to win back your love. I love you very much and I always will. Come with me to England. I cannot bear to be parted from you again.'

Words failed me as I stood glued to the floor. He stood up and led me back to the couch. 'Natalie, please say yes,' he said.

'Oh Tommy, I don't know what to say.'

But deep down inside, I had already made up my mind. For the first time in my life, I had been offered an opportunity to leave Dickson Village. His speech had thrilled me more than any words could say. Images of a new life in England raced around in my head. Then I suddenly remembered Mum. No matter what happened, we always had each other.

As if reading my thoughts, he said, 'Don't worry about your mum, she will be welcome to visit us at any time.' Before I could reply, the lock turned in the door and my little girl entered, shouting happily, 'Mummy, mummy!' Kate and Mum came in behind her.

'Hello darling,' I said, picking her up. On seeing Tommy, Kate quickly about turned, and together Mum and I looked at a puzzled and angry Tommy. I looked at Mum; somehow she guessed that I hadn't told him about his daughter.

'Come on Tina,' she said, extending her arms. Tina went to her. 'Who's that man, Granny? she asked.

'This is Tommy,' she replied.

'Hello Tommy, are you my mum's friend?'

'Yes, I am,' he replied politely.

'You've got freckles like me,' she continued with a little giggle.

'Come on Tina, stop asking so many questions,' said Mum. She greeted Tommy with a hug and kiss, then left the room carrying Tina.

'See you later, Mummy,' Tina shouted. Then Tommy and I were again alone.

'You've got a daughter' he said. 'Natalie, why didn't you tell me?' I didn't reply. 'The child's father?' Still I made no reply. 'Natalie,' he said in a softer tone, 'come on, talk to me.'

I took a deep breath and answered, 'That was Tina.'

'Yes, I know her name,' he replied.

'That was Tina Steinford Harrison, your daughter.'

He broke away from me and took a few steps backwards, stunned.

'My daughter?' he choked. 'How? When?'

'I'm sorry you had to find out this way, Tommy,' I said.

'Why didn't you tell me?'

'Because I wanted you to finish your studies and make us proud.'

'Natalie, I wasn't here for you,' he said softly.

'I was fine, after all I had Mum.'

'Oh Natalie!' he cried. We hugged in silence. Then suddenly he asked, 'What if I had decided not to come back to Dickson Village? Would I have ever known?'

This question took me by surprise, for it had never crossed my mind. I had always known that one day Tommy and I would be reunited.

Just as I was about to reply, our beautiful daughter appeared in the doorway.

'Mummy, I'm tired,' she said, rubbing her eyes.

'Come to Mummy darling,' I said, as she walked towards me.

'Please allow me,' Tommy said as she approached us. He knelt down, beckoning Tina. Puzzled, she looked at me.

'Go on darling, it's OK,' I said to her. I looked at Tommy and for the second time in my life I saw him crying silently. Tina stood still. 'Why is he crying, Mummy?' she asked.

'Because he's very happy,' I replied. 'Now go on, don't be afraid.'

She walked forward and he gently took hold of her hand.

'Hello again, Tina,' he said through his tears.

'You speak funny,' she replied. 'Do you live far away?'

'Yes, I live in England.'

'My daddy lives in England,' she replied. 'Mummy says he's coming back to get us one day.'

I watched in silence as he cuddled his daughter. They were lost in a world of their own. I knew this was the happiest and proudest day of Tommy's life.

'Should we sit down?' I said. We sat down, and on that lovely evening I introduced Tina to her father.

They were both very happy. Tina showered him with questions and I listened as she filled him in on what she had been getting up to in school. Tommy continued holding her tight, as if letting her go would mean losing her again. I excused myself, then left them alone before disappearing around the corner. I looked back and smiled a happy smile, for my daughter had finally got something I also wanted - a father.

That evening Tommy took pleasure in putting Tina to bed, and after reading her a bedtime story she was soon fast asleep. He then rejoined me downstairs.

'What an evening,' he joked.

'There's definitely no argument there,' I replied.

We spent most of the night talking. After all there was so much to talk about. It was my turn to fill him in on all that had been happening in my life. I told him all about Peter in every detail, about my work, my dad, about Betty and her upcoming wedding and the baby and most of all we talked about little Tina. The more my story unfolded before his eyes, the more determined he was for Tina and me to move away with him. I couldn't agree more.

He listened attentively as I spoke and sympathised on many occasions. By the time I was finished I was exhausted but relieved, relieved that I had finally had a chance to share everything with him.

'Life is such a long, long road to travel,' he said, smiling at me as he wrapped his arms even tighter around me. We made ourselves comfortable on the couch, and as exhaustion kicked in, we were soon fast asleep. We decided he would return to England to prepare the paperwork for Tina and me, then we'd follow when everything was finalized. I decided I was going to break the news to Mum the following day over breakfast.

We awoke to the sound of clinking plates and realised that it was morning. 'My god!' I shouted, jumping hastily to my feet, 'what time is it?'

Kate heard me from the kitchen and poked her head round the corner. 'Hello there,' she said. 'Can I get either of you anything before I leave to take Tina to school?'

'No thank you,' we jointly replied, as I led Tommy upstairs towards the bathroom. 'By the way Natalie,' she continued, 'I called your work and told them you're suffering from an upset stomach and hopefully will be fit for work tomorrow.'

'Thanks Kate, you're one in a million.'

Tommy and I showered quickly and arrived downstairs just before she left with an excited Tina. The house was so alive, so happy. I looked at Tommy and his daughter; they were inseparable. She was running after him shouting 'Daddy daddy!' Quietly I watched as they talked and laughter filled the air. Tina was truly in her element. I left them alone after a short while. I had had Tina all to myself from birth, so it was now Tommy's turn to get to know his daughter. I excused myself and joined Kate in the kitchen.

The news of Tommy's return was now all over the village, and villagers dropped in one by one to welcome him home. Dickson Village was so proud of Dr Tommy Harrison. He was someone to look up to.

By the time Mum arrived home, it was late evening and supper had been prepared. She took a few minutes to freshen up, and then we sat down to eat.

'Natalie, you have something to tell me, now what is it?' she said. The room became silent, all eyes focused on me. I was lost for words.

'Come on dear, out with it. What is it?'

'Tommy has asked me to move to England with him and I've said yes,' I said softly. 'That's great,' she replied. 'That's exactly what you and Tina need. A change will do you both good. After all that you've been through Natalie my darling, you need this. I'm so happy for you.'

'Oh Mum!' I cried, searching for her hand from across the table. 'I love you so much. You're so wonderful!'

'Thank you dear,' she said, as she squeezed my hand gently, excused herself and disappeared into the kitchen.

That night I found myself alone in my room, countless questions floating around in my head. Could I ever live without Mum? I had tried once but failed miserably, and now I was going overseas, far, far away. Somewhere she couldn't reach me by car, bus or train.

'Natalie', Tommy called. 'Just a minute,' I answered, as I tidied myself in the mirror.

'Are you all right?' Tommy asked, as I turned the handle and opened the door.

'Yes I'm fine,' I lied.

'Goodnight,' he said, as he kissed me gently and walked towards his room. 'Stop worrying.'

The house was very quiet, too quiet. I stood alone, looking at his closed door and feeling lost. His kiss had been so soft, so warm, so overpowering. I needed to give more. 'Come back,' a voice inside me called quietly. I shivered at the thought of him caressing me, making love to me, taking me to the heights of ecstasy where he had taken me only once before. I stepped back and closed my door as warm juices of pleasure awoke in me.

The next day I returned to work and found myself missing my Tommy terribly. Every second I had spare, I telephoned him.

'You're looking very chirpy today, Natalie,' commented one of the reporters at lunch, 'won the lottery have you?'

'Better than the lottery,' I replied, with a huge smile.

Later that afternoon I called Betty, and told her about Tommy's return and my plans to emigrate. She was very pleased to hear that Tommy and I were reunited and agreed that a change from Dickson was exactly what Tina and I needed. She was busy making final preparations for her big day, which wasn't far away. She was full of excitement and couldn't wait to be Dennis's wife. She complained about the weight she'd gain due to her pregnancy, but she cherished and loved every moment of her new journey, even the morning sickness.

As the days slipped too quickly by I ached, for I knew Tommy's departure was imminent. We were all enjoying his company so much, and we had become one happy family.

Finally the cherished two weeks that we had together ended. Tommy returned to England, and although I knew we were to be reunited soon, this time for life, I hoped, I felt lost and lonely. I counted every minute of every day that we were apart.

CHAPTER 13

MEETING MY FATHER

It was now Betty's and Anthony's double wedding day. The two couples looked gorgeous. I stood by Betty's side and cried with joy, for I was so happy for her. The ceremony was divine, and by the ending, the entire congregation was in tears. As we stood outside the church for photographs I tried to stay back, for it was Betty's big day and I didn't want to crowd her, but she wasn't having any of it. Every move she made, I was ordered to do the same. She shone with sheer radiance, and as I looked at her I couldn't help wishing that it was Tommy and me.

We went to the exquisite Sunset Shores Hotel for the evening reception and Tina and I sat comfortably at Betty's side. When it was time for me to make my speech I spoke from the heart. I spoke about our true and longing friendship, her loyalty and sincerity. The banquet hall's two hundred guests applauded as I concluded with a toast to the newly-weds. As I took my seat, she whispered through happy tears, 'Thank you Natalie.' Then I felt a sense of sadness, as I realised that today was going to be the last day I was going to see her for a while, for by the time she returned from her honeymoon Tina and I would be gone to live in England. Would I get a chance to say a proper goodbye to her before she left? There were so many people wanting her attention tonight that I was certain I wasn't going to get a chance.

After a hearty and enjoyable meal, the music started and the newly-wedded couples took to the dance floor for the first dance. I looked at Betty as she lost herself in Dennis's arms. She caught my smile and I blinked and blew her a kiss. She closed her eyes and rested her head on her husband's shoulder, and for the second time that day I wished it was Tommy and me. To see my best friend so happy was wonderful.

Other couples then took to the dance floor and I joined Mum, who was busy in conversation with Mrs Jackson. I looked around for Tina and found that she too had found herself a little partner and was on the dance floor. This made me chuckle.

'Doesn't she look gorgeous?' Mum said, catching my gaze.

'She certainly does,' I replied.

I looked around the room and saw that everyone was having a wonderful time. Some were on the dance floor, others were busy feeding their faces, while others were busy in conversation - today was indeed a happy day.

Tina, who was now off the dance floor, came running towards me. 'Hello darling,' I said, greeting her, 'are you OK? Oh look, you've spilt the drink on your dress.' She looked at me with cheeky eyes and grinned widely. 'Come on,' I said, 'let me clean you up.'

I took her by the hand and led her to the rest room, where she talked continuously about the day's activities. Then I heard a familiar and welcome voice behind me. 'Aunty Betty!' Tina screamed, running towards her.

'Be careful Tina,' I said, 'you don't want to hurt Aunty Betty now, do you?'

Betty scooped her up and said, 'My god, whatever has your mum been feeding you?'

'Chocolate cookies,' Tina replied, laughing.

'Oh, I'm going to miss you both,' said Betty as she held Tina tight.

'We're going to miss you too,' I replied.

She put Tina down and Betty and I hugged longingly. 'I just thought I'd come and say goodbye now, before I miss my chance,' she cried.

'Oh come on now, don't cry, it's your wedding day, remember.'

She looked at me with sad eyes, then once again took me into her arms. 'Don't forget to write, I want a letter and phone call from you every day,' she said.

'I promise I will.'

There was a knock on the door, and Dennis

shouted, 'Are you in there, Betty? Everyone's asking for you.'

We broke loose, and Betty took a deep breath and answered, 'I'll be out soon.'

'You must go now,' I said to her. Congratulations, by the way, Dennis is a very lucky man.'

'Thanks.' She kissed me again, said goodbye, then left. 'Goodbye Betty,' I shouted after her, 'take great care.' She turned, blew a kiss at me, then disappeared.

There were so many things to be finalised before my departure. Kate and Mum of course lent a helping hand. As the days passed the happier I became, for I was going to be reunited with my Tommy. With four days remaining, I decided it was time for me to contact my father. I was still none the wiser about him, as Mum still refused to talk to me. Whatever was I to say to him?

One afternoon while Mum was out shopping I decided to search her room in an effort to find his address. My hands shook terribly as I made my way for the first time in my life through her personal belongings - to me it was an invasion of her privacy. Nevertheless, it had to be done. I searched and searched, trying desperately to cover my tracks, but all in vain. I had looked everywhere - where could it be?

Eventually I gave up my search, then went back downstairs just before Mum came bursting through the front door carrying bags of shopping.

'Grab this for me please Natalie,' she said, nodding towards her handbag, which was falling loose from beneath her arm. I took the bag and helped her into the kitchen, and then it suddenly dawned on me that the address might be in the bag. I put it on the kitchen table.

'Natalie, how was your day, have you finished all your packing?' she asked.

'Yes,' I replied.

'Are you all right dear?' she asked, looking concerned.

'Yes I'm fine thank you.'

'I'll take these upstairs while you pour me a cool drink,' she said, and she grabbed the bag from the table and left.

I sat in the kitchen for about half an hour, steadied myself, then shouted up to her. There was no reply. I climbed the stairs carrying her drink and entered her bedroom with searching eyes. There was her hand bag sitting on a pile of boxes in the corner.

'Thank you,' she said smiling, 'now have you finished your inspection?'

'I was just wondering why you've packed so many bags when you're only coming with us to England for two weeks.'

'You never did make a good liar,' she replied, pointing towards her two small cases.

'I'm sorry Mum.'

'Never mind.' She placed her now empty glass on the bedside table. 'Now,' she said smiling, 'I believe this is what you've been searching for.' She handed me a sealed envelope.

My hands trembled as I took it from her. I turned

it over and realised it was a letter addressed to me, although I did not recognise the handwriting.

'Go on, open it,' she said. I sat down on her bed before my legs failed me. Slowly and carefully I tore the envelope open. Inside was a letter. I read it out loud.

Dear Natalie,

Never before have I had to write such a difficult letter. I have tried writing to you many times before, but unfortunately in situations like this words are so difficult to find, for what can one say to a daughter (a grown woman) you haven't seen since she was three years old?

Natalie, for reasons beyond my control I've missed out on the most important part of your life, and for this, my daughter, I'm truly sorry.

I hope that some day you will find it in your heart to forgive me. Coming back into your life has been terrifying for both of us. I longed and prayed each day for the opportunity to get to know you and my granddaughter, to know the things you like and dislike. Unfortunately you've clearly stated your wishes and I've accepted and respected your decision. I hope that one day you'll change your mind. I will be waiting. May God continue to bless you, and I wish you good luck in everything you do.

Love always
Percy Steinford (Dad)

I gently stroked my father's handwriting. Mum remained completely still.

'Why was he in prison?' I found myself asking.

'That's a question you'll have to ask him,' she replied.

'Why don't you ever want to talk about him, Mum?'

She remained silent. With that, I left the room, clutching the letter tightly in my hand.

The next day as dawn broke, I was on my way to Baroullie, known as the 'black fish city', on the leeward side of the island, in search of my father. Thousands of questions raced around in my head. What was I to say to him? I knew not. Should I have called first and told him I was on my way? What would his reaction be when he saw me? Questions still tortured me as I reached the village and found his address, after directions from a local street vendor.

I took a deep breath and banged loudly on the door. There was no reply. I knocked again, and a woman's voice answered, 'Just a minute.' A few seconds later the door opened and an elegantly-dressed woman in her sixties stood in the doorway. Her mixture of silver and black short permed hair glistened in the sun.

'Yes,' she said after inspecting me, 'how can I help you?'

'I'm looking for Percy Steinford. I believe he lives here.'

Her eyes searched me again and she asked, 'And you are?'

'I'm sorry,' I said extending my hand, 'I'm Natalie, Natalie Steinford, his daughter.'

'So you're Natalie,' she replied, smiling broadly as she took my hand in hers. 'It's so wonderful to finally meet you. Percy hasn't stopped talking about you. I was beginning to think you were a figment of his imagination. I'm Gertrude, Gertrude Samuel. Do come in.'

I followed her into the well-decorated house and was fascinated by the collection of beautiful paintings hanging from what seemed like every wall. She caught my gaze and said, 'Painting is a hobby of mine, they are all my creations'.

'They're beautiful,' I said, admiring them closely.

'Thank you,' she replied, as she led me through to the front room. 'He'll be back shortly, he's just popped to the shop. Can I get you anything to drink?'

'Yes thanks, a glass of cold water please.'

She fetched the water and we sat down. I felt at ease, for she was so easy to talk to, so welcoming, friendly and hospitable.

About half an hour later the key turned in the door and a man's voice yelled, 'Gertrude I'm back.' My heart raced as his footsteps grew louder and louder, closer and closer. I jumped to my feet. 'Gertrude,' he called again, 'are you at home?'

'I'm in the front room,' she replied, smiling at me. I took a deep breath and clasped my hands together tightly. I was a nervous wreck.

Then Percy Steinford came in, newspaper in hand. He stopped and stood staring at me in shock. Gertrude's footsteps broke the silence as she left the room.

'Hello Dad,' I said.

'Hello Natalie,' he replied. 'How's your mum?'

'She's fine.'

'And Tina, how is she?'

'Very naughty,' I smiled.

The wrinkles on his aged face increased as his smile broadened. I began to feel at ease, for his smile was so much like Tina's.

He opened his arms and I flew into them. It felt wonderful and I was trembling with excitement. All my life I had dreamt of this moment. To have a dad, my very own daddy! My dream had finally come true. I had a father at last.

The more we talked, the more at ease I felt. He seemed so shy and lovable. With deep sorrow I listened as he told the story of his unhappy past. I learnt that Mum and Dad had been childhood sweethearts. Mum, an only child, had lived with her father and Grandpa Jones. Her mum had died from cancer when she was only twelve years old, and they were very poor. Her dad had died a year later of a broken heart.

Dad, on the other hand, came from a very wealthy family who disliked Mum. Unfortunately Mum got pregnant with me at sixteen, and this brought disgrace to Dad's side of the family. Because of the love they had for each other my parents ran away and set up home together. They lived in poverty, but they were very happy as they found all the wealth they needed in each other. When Mum turned eighteen they got married. Dad never contacted his side of the family, but Grandpa Jones stuck by them.

Just after my third birthday Dad's parents discovered our whereabouts. Grandpa Jones, Mum's only living relative, was staying with us at the time. I was at playgroup. It was then that disaster struck. They ordered my dad to take me, leave my mum behind and return with them, but he refused. After a lengthy argument my grandfather asked Dad's parents to leave, as he found their comments rude and insulting. They refused. In anger Grandpa Jones decided to grab both Dad's parents and pushed them towards the door. Dad's mum slipped and fell to the floor, and there was a scuffle between my grandfathers. Dad separated them, shouting that he would return home with his parents.

Mum stood in tears shocked and confused. This irritated Grandpa Jones even more, and he launched himself at Dad with all his might. Dad pushed him away and Grandpa fell backwards, hitting his head on the edge of the coffee table. He died instantly.

'Oh my god, why wasn't I told any of this?' I cried. 'How could Mum keep all this from me?'

I looked deep into his eyes and felt the sadness as he cried floods of tears. I was hurting as I discovered my father had been convicted of manslaughter, not accidental death - hurting to know that mum had never stood by him, she was not present in court and not once did she visit him in prison. She had just taken me and disappeared.

'Don't be angry with your mum, Natalie,' he said, as if reading my thoughts. 'She did the right thing. My parents would have done everything in their power to take you away from her, I was so happy when she couldn't be found.'

'Were you really going to go back with your parents and leave us behind?' I asked.

'Of course not, I only said that to defuse the situation. You and your mum were my life, you were all that I wanted.'

'How did you find us?'

'Your mum and I always talked about moving to Dickson Village. In my heart I always knew that's where she'd gone.'

Gertrude entered the room carrying light refreshments, then left again. Dad and I continued talking for hours; there was so much to talk about, so much for us to learn about each other. I told him all about Tina and Tommy and my move to England. This saddened him, to find that after waiting years to find me I was now going across the Atlantic to live thousands of miles away. I reassured him that I would keep in regular contact and that he was welcome to visit at any time.

That night I found it impossible to sleep, for echoes of my dad's voice raced around inside my head. I thought hard about my grandparents and my other living relatives, then about Mum. How could she not tell me any of these things, how had she kept such a secret for so many years? I became angry, troubled and confused. I was restless, and for the entire night not once did I close my eyes.

Before I knew it the cockerels were crowing, the farmhands were on their way to work and the sun was rising; it was morning. I looked at my untouched overnight bag on the chair opposite me and sighed a sad sigh.

An hour later I was refreshed, changed and had arrived downstairs for breakfast.

'Morning,' I shouted to Dad and Gertrude, as I joined them at the table.

'Good morning, did you sleep OK?' Dad asked, looking concerned.

'Fine thanks,' I lied. We talked through breakfast, for there were still so many questions I had to ask, and he took pleasure in answering them. A few hours later, as we said our farewells, he made me promise not to upset Mum on my return, for he strongly believed that she had done the right thing.

I drove back with many questions swimming around inside my head. How could I face Mum after all that I had heard? I knew things would never be the same between us again. I smiled at the thought of meeting my new relatives. What were they like, I wondered? To meet them, to talk to them, my grandparents and more, how exciting.

I arrived home and parked the car. Mum noticed me through the window and waved. My heart began to race. I stood still and took a deep breath before I opened the door. I walked slowly through the house, dumping my travel bag at the bottom of the stairs.

'You're back then,' Mum said from behind me. My body shook like a leaf blowing in the wind, for I was getting set for round two. I turned in her direction and stood looking at her, lost for words.

'How are you?' she asked. I wanted to reply, but words failed me. Her wrinkled face grew dim as her smile faded. 'The packing's completed and tickets collected,' she continued. 'We're all set for our journey. By the way, Tommy called.' With that she was gone.

I remained rooted to the ground, lost in a daze. Some time later I picked my bag up and headed to my room. Tomorrow was a big day, for I was leaving to be reunited with Tommy.

Relaxed at last, I looked around the untidy room. I smiled as I spotted my packed cases resting in the corner. My eyes came to a halt on the dressing table, for there standing all alone was a photograph of Mum, Tina and me, taken at Christmas two years before. I gazed at the three happy faces and remembered the day it had been taken, and slowly I drifted back to the many happy years all three of us had shared. Dad's voice reminded me not to upset Mum. I looked at her broad smile in the picture. How was I to approach her? All through the years talking to her had been so easy. I had thought I knew everything, but I was so wrong.

'Whatever I did, I did it for you,' Mum said, as she put her head through the door. 'It was my only way of protecting you.'

I looked up as she approached me. 'I thought we always talked about everything,' I managed to reply.

'Natalie, I so wanted to tell you the truth, but I convinced myself that the past had never happened, after all I was so happy with the present.'

She sat beside me and I listened in silence as she confirmed everything Dad had told me the night before. I tried to imagine what it must have been like for her, a young girl and daughter on the run from her husband's family in an effort to keep hold of her only child. I took her trembling hand into mine and asked, 'Why didn't you visit him in prison?'

'I couldn't, I was too scared.'

We sat in silence for a while. Then she asked, 'Your dad, how is he?'

'He seems OK,' I replied. 'He's upset of course about my moving away.'

'I've never stopped loving him,' she whispered softly. I looked at her, for I did not know what to say. This had taken me completely by surprise.

'We had some fun together, your dad and I,' she continued with a smile. 'No matter what his parents did or said we always found a way to be together.'

'Oh Mum,' I said, rubbing her hands gently.

'I was so happy to see him that day when he turned up at the shop, surprised but very happy. Apart from a few wrinkles he hadn't changed one bit.' Her eyes sparkled. She twisted her wedding band, which she had never taken off from the day it had been placed on her finger so many years ago.

We rocked quietly from side to side. I sighed, in relief this time, for it felt great to be close to Mum again.

CHAPTER 14

THE DEPARTURE

It was my final morning in Dickson Village, and I awoke as dawn broke. The thought of seeing Tommy in a matter of hours filled my heart with joy. I was dressed and ready for my journey when Timothy, our local taxi driver, came to collect us. I arrived outside to find a group of locals offering their good wishes. Mum and Tina were already in their midst, trying desperately to comfort a tearful Kate.

'It's time to go,' said Timothy, as I joined them.

I felt like royalty that day as we drove off slowly through the village. Passing villagers waved at us. As we approached the end of the village, I shouted, 'Can you please stop here for a minute Timothy?' The car stopped, and they all looked at me with puzzled eyes.

I turned around in my seat and took one last look at Dickson Village. I could still see a few villagers.

I closed my eyes and said a quick prayer. I asked God to guide and protect us, and to bring us back home again safely some day.

'We've got to get going, Natalie,' Timothy interrupted. I opened my eyes, took one final look at the village and said out loud, 'Goodbye Dickson Village, see you again someday.' Then we were on our way.

We arrived at the airport to find Dad and Gertrude waiting. Although it had not been long, I was ecstatic to see him. We hugged each other tightly and I whispered, 'Thanks for coming Dad, this really means a lot to me.'

'My pleasure,' he replied as we separated. I hugged Gertrude as he took Tina into his arms. Quietly I watched as he exchanged a few words with Mum and Timothy.

'Dad, I've got something for you,' I said.

'This must be my lucky day, what is it?'

I took off the golden necklace given to me by Mum on my graduation day and passed it to him. He opened the locket, looked at the picture of Mum and me and said, 'Natalie, I can't take this.'

'Of course you can,' I replied. 'It was given to me by someone I love truly and now I want to give it to you, for that someone not only means a lot to me, she means a lot to you too. Now allow me.'

I took the necklace from him and placed it around his neck. 'Thank you,' he said. Then a familiar voice shouted from behind me, 'Hello Natalie'.

I turned around to face an excited Betty. 'Oh my god Betty, what are you doing here?' I screamed. 'You're supposed to be on your honeymoon.'

'I just had to come and say goodbye,' she replied as we embraced.

'Hello Natalie,' another familiar voice said. I looked up and saw Dennis, Betty's husband, and the rest of her family walking towards me. There were hugs and showers of kisses, introductions were made to Dad and Gertrude and before I knew it, it was time to leave.

'Well, this is it,' I said. 'Thanks to all of you for coming to see us off.'

'We just wanted to make sure you were definitely leaving,' Anthony teased. 'Peace at last.' I laughed and said, 'I'll miss you all very much.'

Betty held me tight. 'Please keep in touch, I'm going to miss you so much,' she cried.

'Please look after Betty and the baby,' I called to Dennis over her shoulder.

'My greatest pleasure,' he replied.

Mum tapped me gently. It was time to go. 'Goodbye all,' I yelled, 'and thanks again.'

As Mum, Tina and I walked off leaving them all behind, a great feeling of sadness overpowered me, but I fought hard to hold back the tears, for I knew that if I started I would find it impossible to stop. I looked down at a happy Tina and smiled. I wanted desperately to look back, but didn't.

'Goodbye Natalie,' Betty shouted before we disappeared. I lifted my hand high above my head and without turning around I replied, 'Goodbye, see you all soon.' With that we were gone, leaving our group of sobbing relations (for they were all our relations) behind.

We arrived in England after a long and tiring journey on a very cold winter's morning. Never before had I felt such cold, and I shivered as I emerged from the plane carrying Tina. We got safely through customs, and as we walked with other passengers through the huge airport I was overcome with excitement. We stopped to buy some duty-free perfume, then we walked through a large door and arrived at the arrival lounge where family and friends were waiting to greet their loved ones.

My eyes searched for Tommy. 'Calm down dear,' Mum whispered, noticing my anxiety. She tapped me on the shoulder and my eyes followed her pointing finger directly to Tommy. Bunch of flowers and teddy bear in hand, he stood amongst the crowd. His freckled face shone brightly as his eyes caught mine. As we approached him, he burst into laughter.

'Welcome to England!' he said, as he clasped me tightly to his chest.

'Daddy, Daddy!' a happy Tina called.

'Hello, my little princess,' he replied, as he broke away from me and scooped her up. He kissed her repeatedly. 'Hello Mrs Steinford,' he said, greeting Mum, 'it's wonderful to see you again.'

So on that cold winter's day Tina and I began our new life in the United Kingdom. I was so happy, because my family was now complete.

It's amazing how when you're having fun, you lose your grip on reality. The two weeks Mum spent with us were blissful, but unfortunately before long it was time for her to leave. Tommy and I took her to the airport and after a tearful farewell my mother was gone.

As we drove back from the airport I felt nostalgic for the first time since my arrival.

'What am I going to do without Mum?' I found myself asking out loud.

'You'll be fine,' Tommy replied. You and Tina are now my responsibility, forever.' I smiled a shy but satisfied smile.

CHAPTER 15

THE PROPOSAL

The months went speedily by. I got a secretarial job for the local newspaper, Tina was enrolled in school and Tommy was great, life was perfect. As a family, every moment spent together was truly accounted for. Tina and I adapted to our new life with ease. I kept in touch with everyone back home. I was very pleased to learn that Mum and Dad were getting on well, and was overjoyed when they rang a few months later to say that they were now living together.

It was the middle of summer. One evening as I was getting ready to attend a barbecue at Tommy's Mum's house, I felt queasy. I sat on the edge of the bath and looked at my happy face in the mirror, for I was indeed very happy, having been to the doctor's the day before and listened as he confirmed my suspicion that I was indeed pregnant.

'Natalie?' Tommy called to me. 'Tina and I will be in the car.'

'OK,' I replied as I steadied myself. I would tell Tommy the good news on our return.

We arrived at Mrs Harrison's house and as she opened the front door, I couldn't help but noticing how radiant she looked. I reflected back to the way she had looked before she left Dickson Village, so many years ago. I excused myself and went to the bathroom.

'Your trips to the bathroom are becoming very frequent,' Tommy teased me from behind.

'Too much to drink, dear,' I replied before disappearing round the corner. I returned and as I entered the garden, I noticed a group of people surrounding Tommy. He saw me and beckoned for me to join him. I did so and he proudly put his hand around me while introductions were made.

Mrs Harrison, I noticed, was now doing what she did best, mingling with a group of gentlemen guests, Tina by her side. I smiled at her, for she was being outrageously flirtatious.

Just then I noticed a well-dressed young man walking towards us; he was tall, blonde and slim.

'Tommy, you old devil,' he said as he approached us, 'I'm sorry I'm late.'

'Derrick! I hadn't forgotten for one moment how good you are at time keeping,' Tommy replied.

'I see you haven't lost your sense of humour,' the newcomer replied, extending his hand. I stepped backwards as they both got lost in conversation. I began to feel uncomfortable as questions began to race around in my head. Why hadn't Tommy mentioned Derrick before? Who was he? Was history repeating itself? My stomach tightened at these thoughts. I excused myself and raced for the bathroom.

I was paranoid, very paranoid. I splashed my face with water and gazed with wondering eyes into the mirror, seeing images of Peter and Robert.

'Is something the matter, young woman?' a woman asked from the opened door.

'No, I'm fine thanks,' I lied. She hesitated for a moment, looked at me, then left. I took a deep breath, tidied myself, reapplied my make-up, then rejoined the group outside. By this time Tina and Mrs Harrison had joined it.

'Have you been crying, Natalie?' Tommy asked. 'Your eyes looked rather puffed.'

'No, I'm just feeling a bit tired that's all.'

'Living with you is enough to bring anyone to tears,' Derrick joked, winking at me.

'Natalie, this is Derrick, he used to be my roommate when I was at university,' said Tommy. 'Derrick, meet Natalie, my girlfriend and the mother of my beautiful daughter Tina.'

Derrick extended his hand and smiled broadly. He took my hand in his, kissed it gently and said, 'It is an absolute pleasure to meet you, you are as beautiful as Tommy described.'

'Thank you,' I replied, 'it's a pleasure to meet you too.'

We chatted for a while and the more I spoke to Derrick, the more I got to like him. He was simply charming. I learnt that he was married and the proud father of triplets, three beautiful girls to whom Tommy was godfather.

'There you are,' a voice interrupted, I've been looking everywhere for you.' Together we turned to face the young lady I had met in the toilet doorway earlier. I watched as he kissed her gently then said, 'Natalie, this is my wife Nina.'

'Hello, nice to meet you.' We shook hands and she smiled.

Nina and I got more acquainted and I listened as she talked with pride about her children. I felt comfortable with her, for she reminded me so much of Betty. She had a charming personality, a great sense of humour and most of all she had Betty's giggle.

'Nina, do you mind if I steal her away from you for a minute?' Tommy interrupted.

'No, not at all,' Nina replied.

'Excuse me Nina, I'll see you later,' I said. Tommy took hold of my hand and led me into the house, then through to the huge lounge.

'Where's Tina?' I asked.

'She's with Mum, I just wanted to be on my own for a few minutes with you.'

'Dirty devil,' I said, as he pulled me close.

'Here, sit down,' he said, leading me to the chair. Together we sat and he wrapped his arm around me. I gazed into his sparkling eyes. It was a warm summer's evening and the trees stood still for there wasn't even the slightest breeze.

I looked deep into his eyes as our lips met in the most passionate kiss ever. We kissed longingly. Had it been somewhere else, I believe we would have ventured further.

'I love you, Natalie,' he whispered.

'I love you too Tommy.'

'Natalie - will you marry me?'

I was lost for words. The question I had been waiting to hear had finally been asked.

'Yes,' I replied without hesitation, 'Yes, yes, yes!'

Our lips met hungrily. Then he broke off. 'Just a minute, I must do this properly,' he said. I watched with excitement as he produced a ring from his pocket, knelt down before me and asked once again, 'Natalie Steinford, will you marry me?'

And on that warm summer's evening, I once again gladly shouted, 'Yes, yes, yes, I will!'

As we rejoined the party, Tina came running towards us.

'How's my little beauty?' Tommy asked, taking hold of her hand.

'Fine, thank you,' she replied.

'So you two have finally decided to join us,' Derrick said as we approached the still-gathered group. Together Tommy and I laughed.

'Derrick mate, we've got some good news,' said Tommy. His eyes sparkled as he looked at the anxious eyes of our friends.

'Well, aren't you going to share it with us?' said Derrick.

'Yes,' Tommy replied, taking hold of my hand. 'Natalie has agreed to be my wife.'

The group showered us with kisses and congratulations. 'Well,' Derrick said after a short while, 'we must drink a toast to Natalie and Tommy, if you can all raise your glasses.'

'Hang on, there's something I'd like to say,' I said. I felt Tommy's grip on my hand tighten as he adjusted Tina, now asleep on his shoulders. Wide eyes looked at me in anticipation. 'I'm not sure if this is the right time to say this, but I'm saying it anyway, after all the excitement of what's turned out to be the happiest day of my life I'm proud and very happy to say that Tommy and I are expecting another baby.'

'We are?' Tommy blurted out in shock.

'Yes darling,' I replied with a smile. We kissed and the crowd around us clapped. The toast was proposed and the evening ended beautifully.

We arrived home, and immediately I was on the phone to Mum and Dad to share my double news. They were both very happy for me and couldn't wait for the big day. I then phoned Betty. Like my parents Betty was happy for me and we talked for hours as usual.

As the weeks went by my stomach grew larger and larger. We planned to get married a month before the baby was born. Tina was very happy about the thought of having a little brother or sister; she was developing beautifully into a little madam.

One evening I arrived to pick her up from school as I always did, but she was not at the school gates where she and her friend Sarah always waited for me. I parked the car and waited for about twenty minutes, for I thought that they were late coming out. I waited and waited, but still there was no sign of either of them. Where could she be?

I locked the car and walked carefully up the school steps, then into the school.

'Can I help you?' a voice asked. I turned to my left to see one of the teachers, who had obviously stayed late.

'Yes,' I replied, 'I'm looking for my daughter, Tina Steinford Harrison.'

'I don't think there's anyone here except the cleaners,' the teacher replied.

My entire body shook as I began to imagine the worst. We searched the school, but there was no sign of Tina or Sarah. The teacher led me to the office, reassuring me that the girls were probably safe at home.

I used the office phone and called home, but there was no answer. I headed hastily to my car, the teacher on my tail. I called Tommy at work and within minutes he was by my side, even more shaken than I was. As I saw him running towards me I broke down. 'My baby, my little baby!' I cried. He held me close in an effort to console me. Then the police arrived along with the head teacher. Sarah's parents arrived a few minutes later.

I was advised to go home and wait for the girls while the police conducted their search. Tommy stayed behind. As I arrived home, Glenda, our full-time housekeeper, met me at the front door. 'Any news?' I asked.

'I'm afraid not.' She took hold of my hand and led me into the house.

I sat by the telephone and waited and waited, but it did not ring.

'I can't bear this any more!' I screamed, jumping to my feet. 'My daughter is out there somewhere and I am going to find her.'

'Natalie please,' Glenda begged, 'considering your condition, you must rest.'

'I'm sorry Glenda, I can't rest, I really can't, not while my daughter is out there.'

Just then a car pulled up outside, and together we ran to the door. It was Tommy, looking completely exhausted. I ran towards him.

'Tommy, where is she?' I shouted. Before he could reply I felt a sharp pain and fell to the floor in agony. I cried out loud, then the rest was blank.

I awoke in the hospital some hours later to find Tommy by my bedside.

'Hello darling,' I said, trying to sit upright.

'No you mustn't, just lie still.'

Then I remembered Tina. 'My god, Tina! Have they found her?'

'Yes,' he replied. 'She's outside waiting to see her mummy.'

'Oh thank god! That's such a relief. And what about Sarah? What happened to them?'

'They went to the city centre after school. The police picked them up a few hours ago, waiting for the bus to come back.'

'Are they all right?'

'She's fine, don't you worry, I'll fetch her for you.'

I watched as he walked towards the door and beckoned for Tina. A moment later my daughter appeared in the doorway, still in her school uniform. Tears of joy flowed from my eyes as she ran towards me, and I wrapped my arms tenderly around her.

'I'm sorry Mummy, I'm really sorry,' she cried.

'It's OK dear,' I cried, as I kissed her repeatedly.

I was hospitalized for a week as the doctors kept me in for observation and rest. I hated that week, for it dragged slowly by and I was dreadfully bored. Tina spent as much time as she could by my bedside, for she blamed herself for my fall. Finally I was discharged, and I arrived home to find that the house looked like a florist's shop with fresh flowers everywhere. Their fresh scent filled the air.

That evening Tommy invited Derrick and his family over for supper, and it was great seeing them again. Nina glowed with radiance. The meal was served, Glenda's specially made spaghetti bolognese, and even the kids cleaned their plates.

Tommy insisted that I was to stay off work until the baby was born and after countless arguments I finally gave in and agreed that it was the best thing to do. I hated lazing around the house. There was nothing at all to do, as Glenda did it all. My stomach grew bigger and bigger. I started preparations for the wedding, which was now only a few months away. Tommy was full of excitement. It felt great to know that I would soon become Mrs Natalie Harrison.

CHAPTER 16

THE WEDDING

Today was my big day. I stood in front of the mirror dressed in a long diamante-covered ivory off-the-shoulder dress.

'Wow, you look beautiful,' Mum said from behind me as she stroked a strand of hair into place.

'Thank you,' I replied, turning in her direction. She was dressed in an elegant soft pink gown, and I looked at the joy in her eyes.

'I have waited a long time for this day,' she said, as she held my hand, 'and now it has arrived, I am so happy for you.' My tears began to well up. 'Tommy is a very lucky man,' she added. I felt the warmth of my tears as they ran down my face.

'Now now now,' she said, wiping my face gently, 'you must stop. You're ruining your makeup.'

'I'm sorry Mum, I'm so happy.'

We were interrupted by a knock. 'Come in,' said Mum. The handle turned, the door flew open and Betty came in, took one look at me and asked, 'What are you crying for? We spent ages getting your make-up right.' I smiled a faint smile. 'Now that's better,' she said as she hugged me.

There was another knock on the door and Kate joined us. 'Your limousine's just arrived,' she said.

'Thanks Kate,' I replied over Betty's shoulder as she tried to put the finishing touches to my make-up.

The wedding ceremony was breathtakingly beautiful. As Dad walked me down the aisle towards Tommy I felt nervous as all eyes were on me, but as we approached Tommy and Dad handed me over to him I felt happy and confident. Tina waved at me and I could see that Mum, who was sitting beside her, was now in tears.

As we exchanged vows, my entire body shook with emotion. I looked Tommy deep into his eyes and proudly said, 'I do.' A few minutes later I was Mrs Natalie Harrison, and as Tommy and I kissed in the presence of our invited guests I was ecstatic, for at last we were one.

'I love you, Natalie Harrison,' he said as our lips parted.

'I love you too,' I replied as we turned to face a cheerful and teary crowd.

The baby was now only a few weeks away, so we

decided to put off our honeymoon to the following year. Tommy took a couple of weeks off work. Mum and Dad decided to stay until the baby was born before they returned home. Betty and Dennis, on the other hand, only stayed a week, as they had to return for business.

That week we all spent together was magical. My godson Danny was so much like Betty, full of life. His soft curly black hair was brushed neatly into place, he was tall and slim and won Tina over with his shy smile. As Betty introduced us, he hung his head and toyed with his fingers. I was glad that I finally had the opportunity to meet him. His parents cherished him dearly.

Two weeks after Betty, Kate and her family left, I gave birth to another beautiful baby girl, Justina Steinford Harrison. She weighed seven pounds and was in great health. An excited Tommy was present at the birth and held my hand tightly to the end. My parents were proud of their new granddaughter, and as for Tina, she was overjoyed.

A couple of days later I was discharged from the hospital, and when I arrived home Mum, Tina and Glenda took full charge of Justina. They spoilt her rotten, and every time she cried or even tried to make a sound, she was picked up and comforted. I complained frequently, but my words fell on deaf ears.

On the day before my parents returned home, Glenda and Tina took Mum into town for a bit of last-minute shopping. Dad stayed behind. I joined him in the front room, where he was wrapped up in television.

'Fancy a cuppa?' I asked, as I entered the room.'

'Already made,' he replied, pointing to two freshly-made cups of tea on the coffee table. I planted a kiss on his cheek. 'Thanks, you're a darling,' I said.

I sat down beside him as he switched the television off, and we talked for what seemed like hours. I was happy that I had got the opportunity to know my father, and sitting with him and talking to him filled my heart with great joy.

As we talked, the conversation drifted to my grandparents. I became more intrigued, for I wanted so much to know more about them, my family whom I had never met, never known existed. There was a long pause as my thoughts drifted.

'The day I was sentenced I broke my parents' hearts by asking them never to visit me in prison,' said Dad. 'I just couldn't do it to them. They were great parents. Growing up, I wanted for nothing, and during my trial they were so supportive. I never sent them a visiting order or wrote to them. They wrote to me every week, and not once did I reply. I wanted to reply, but I was ashamed, I felt as though I had let them down, they had such hopes for me. When I was released my only aim was to find you and your mother. When I finally contacted my parents and went home, they hugged me and cried for joy.'

My eyes were now quite swollen up and sore, as Dad continued.

'Mum has cervical cancer, and the doctors have given her a few months to live,' he said. I held his hand as he continued, 'I've told them about you, Tina,

Justina and Tommy. Natalie, you're their only grandchild. The last time they saw you, you were three years old. I would like you to meet Mum soon, before she passes away.'

I was lost for words. 'Why didn't you tell me any of this before?' I asked.

'I didn't want to upset you, with the pregnancy, marriage and everything else.'

That night as Tommy and I lay in bed I told him everything. We decided that I was to follow my parents a few weeks later back home to St Vincent and the Grenadines. Tommy had various commitments he couldn't get out of, so he was staying behind, while I was to take Tina and Justina. The thought of seeing the land of my birth, of arriving in Dickson Village to see my friends and the villagers again, to eat the local produce I so longed for, overwhelmed me with joy.

The next day I told my parents of my plans, and Dad was ecstatic. I then phoned an overjoyed Betty, who promised to meet me at the airport.

As I said my goodbyes to my parents at the airport I had no feeling of sadness, for I knew I was seeing them again in a matter of weeks. On my return, Tina, who had packed the day I had told her we were going on holiday, entered my bedroom, where I was busy folding some clothes, and said, 'Mum, I'm just going to walk Sarah home'.

'OK,' I replied, 'don't be long, you have homework to do.'

'OK Mum,' she replied as she ran to join Sarah,

who was waiting downstairs. I listened as they ran hurriedly down the steps. I walked over to my window and drew back the curtain and watched as they walked merrily together, lost in conversation. They reminded me so much of Tommy and me when we were kids.

I closed my eyes and imagined that I was a child again, ten years old and back in Dickson Village. It was a Saturday afternoon, and I felt happy because I didn't have school. I was standing on the front porch, two home-made tamarind balls in hand, waiting for Tommy. Then there he was.

'Natalie!' he shouted as we ran towards each other. As I approached him, I kicked him on the leg. 'Ouch!' he cried in his sweet West Indian accent, 'ah wey yo kick me fah?'

'Fo thievin' me marble yesterday,' I replied, with a wide grin. He put his hand in his pocket and produced my marble.

'Thanks,' I said, as I grabbed it from him. I handed him one of the tamarind balls. The blended flavour of sour and sweet made our eyes water.

'Friends fo' eva,' I said to a teary Tommy.

'Friends fo' eva.' he replied as he kicked me and shouted 'me geh yo back' before running full speed down the road.

'Me gwine ketch yo, Tommy Harrison!' I screamed as I ran to catch him.

CHAPTER 17

HOME SWEET HOME

It was a warm Friday evening when we arrived in St Vincent and the Grenadines. As I stepped down from the plane I looked around and gave a broad and satisfied smile, for there was no place like home. As the sea breeze welcomed me I stood still and took a deep breath, trying to inhale as much of the pure air as I possibly could.

'Home sweet home,' I whispered softly.

I looked down at Justina, who was strapped to my chest in a baby carrier, and removed her hat.

'Come on Mum!' an excited Tina shouted, pulling me along. We made our way slowly through immigration, then to the arrival lounge, where a large group of happy faces greeted us.

Dickson Village remained unchanged. The entire village and its people were exactly the same - warm and tranquil. It was great to be home, and I settled back in with ease. My only wish was to have Tommy with me. Tina made friends easily and I could see that she was enjoying being spoilt by the villagers. I wasted no time in visiting my grandparents.

On day two, I was sitting with Tina and Justina on the back seat of Dad's car, on our way to Lodge Village. After a drive of an hour and a half, Dad finally said, 'We're here.'

I took a deep breath as we all got out of the car. I stood for a moment admiring my grandparents' huge house. I adjusted Justina in my arms and followed Dad and Tina up the many steps.

Dad was about to open the door when a smartly-dressed elderly gentleman appeared, and shouted, 'Hello all, come in. Mrs Steinford caught a cold a few days ago, but she's bearing up.'

I stepped inside the house, still admiring its vastness and the expensive décor. My eyes stopped on a picture of me, Tommy and the kids. Beside it hung what seemed to be a family tree, and a photograph Dad had obviously taken when he had stayed with us in England.

We entered the huge front room as Dad turned to the gentleman who welcomed us and asked, 'How are you, Vibert?'

'I'm bearing up considering,' he replied. Turning to me, Dad said, 'This is Vibert, our neighbour. Vibert and his wife have been employed by my parents since before I was born. Vibert, this is my daughter Natalie and her children.'

Just then footsteps could be heard racing around the corner, and then what looked like an older version of my father entered the room. He stood looking at us all with a broad grin.

'Hello Percy,' he said, shaking Dad's hand. Then he walked towards me with a warm smile. 'Natalie, my granddaughter! At last, it's such a joy to finally meet you.' We embraced.

'Hello Granddad,' I said, laughing wholeheartedly. We hugged for ages, for Granddad didn't want to let me go.

My grandfather was very pleasant and relaxed, taking to Tina and Justina with ease. The more I spoke to him, the more relaxed I felt, and soon it was as if I had known him all my life. My grandmother was asleep, so we had lunch. Everything had already been prepared for us by Vibert and his wife. Lunch was light and delicious; my favourite meal, roasted breadfruit and brown stewed chicken back served with avocado and washed down with a fresh glass of sour sop juice.

After lunch we settled down on the front porch, and I looked around in satisfaction at the beautiful scenic surroundings. Vibert said through the window, 'She's awake.' My grandfather took hold of my hand and said, 'She's going to be so happy to finally meet you, Natalie, thanks for coming.'

'It's my pleasure Granddad. I'm really glad I came.'

As we entered the large bedroom Dad took Justina. Together we all flocked around the king-size carved mahogany four-poster bed. As I looked down at my grandmother, sadness overpowered me. She lay heavily sedated for the pain of the cancer and clearly dying, lost between what seemed like huge sheets, for she was so small, so thin, yet she managed a faint smile. She could hardly keep her eyes open.

Dad kissed her gently and Granddad took her hand in his. 'Natalie and the kids are here, honey,' he said. She opened her eyes slightly and glanced around in satisfaction before closing them again. I took hold of her other hand as I sat down beside her, and tears filled my eyes.

'Hello Grandma,' I choked. I felt a slight pressure as she feebly tried to squeeze my hand. Tears rolled from the corners of her eyes as she tried to mumble something. I kissed her repeatedly. Then she drifted back to sleep. I stayed behind as the rest of the family left the room.

I looked down at my grandmother's frail body and wondered what she had been like when she was younger. Then I began to talk to her, and for some reason, I thought she was listening. I told her all about Tommy and the girls. I told her about living in England and how good it felt to be home, and finally how great it was to finally meet her and Granddad. I chatted to her continuously for hours; after all she had missed out on the whole of my life.

Eventually Dad arrived, pushed his head through the doorway and asked, 'Are you OK in here? Before I could reply, Grandma began coughing uncontrollably. Dad rushed to her and lifted her head slightly as I rubbed her back. The others quickly joined us. Granddad tried wetting her dried lips with a piece of cotton wool soaked in water. But the coughing continued.

'Phone the doctor!' Dad shouted. 'You'll find the number in my study, to the left of this room.' Quickly I rushed from the room, found the number for their private doctor and dialled. The echoes of my beating heart took over as I replaced the phone receiver.

Grandma's cough rang out loudly through the house, then suddenly there was silence. With trembling hands and knees, I entered the quiet bedroom. Everyone looked numb, and my grandfather looked as though he had aged by another fifteen or more years. Dad looked up at me and whispered, 'She's gone.'

Tina ran towards me. I stood motionless hugging her. I couldn't cry. My grandmother had waited so long to meet me.

The funeral was such a sad occasion. My grandfather cried himself tearless. Oh how I felt for him, for he had loved her so much. The ceremony at the church was beautiful. A mixture of fresh flowers decorated the coffin. The church was packed with mourners old and young. Every seat was taken, and even the doorways and street were packed. I sat by my grandfather's side and took his hand in mine, for he looked weak and frail.

After the lengthy service my grandmother was laid to rest in a cemetery nearby. I stood over her grave and looked down at her coffin, and for the first time since her death I began to cry. I fumbled with the red rose I was holding, and as I threw it into the grave I whispered, 'Goodbye Grandma, rest in peace.' I had found my grandmother only to lose her on the same day.

We left the cemetery still full of mourners and headed back with Betty and the rest of the family to my grandparents' house where a wake was being held. I poured myself a much-needed glass of rum punch, then joined Mum and Dad, who were so deep in conversation they didn't see me standing behind them. I looked around the large room, which had been decorated for the occasion. I took in the expressions of sympathy on everyone's faces, the mixture of black and white clothing, the huge black hats the women wore, the children as they ran around trying to keep themselves entertained. Then at the doorway my eyes halted, and I quickly put my empty glass down on the table beside me and leapt forward with joy, shouting 'Tommy, Tommy, Tommy!'

How wonderful it was to see Tommy, for I had missed him so much. We clung on to each other. I wanted him to meet my grandfather, but he was asleep, exhausted after a very long day.

The wake went on for hours. Finally Tommy rejoined me, and I asked, 'Where are your cases?'

'I left them on the porch,' he replied smiling.

I led him into the kitchen. 'Are you hungry? I asked.

'No, just tired.'

'You must be, after your long journey. I'll borrow Dad's car and we'll go home. I'll go and get the keys.'

I returned a few minutes later with the keys and the kids. We said our goodnights to the family and went towards the car. I strapped the kids safely in the back. I was about to sit in the driver's seat when Dad called, 'Natalie, your grandfather is asking for you, he wants to see you.'

I felt that I couldn't leave without saying goodnight to Granddad, so I turned to Tommy and asked, 'Are you OK to drive?'

'Yes I'm fine.' he replied.

'OK you go ahead, take the kids home and I'll come back in an hour with Betty.'

We kissed gently. I kissed and said goodbye to the girls, and I stood waving as Tommy drove off, making funny faces at me in the rear view mirror.

I sat down beside my grandfather and he took my hand in his. He looked so frail, so exhausted. He was lost in a world of his own, and soon he was again asleep. The room was quiet. I felt lost looking at his tired and lonely body and my heart ached. I kicked off my shoes and climbed into bed beside him. I threw my arms around him and in no time I too fell asleep.

Some time later I awoke to find Mum and Dad standing over me. 'What time is it?' I mumbled sleepily. There was no reply. Yawning widely and rubbing my eyes, I forced myself upright and looked up. Two troubled faces looked down at me.

'What is it, what's wrong?' I asked.

'Natalie,' Dad said holding my hand. Mum began to cry.

'For Christ's sake, what is it?' I shouted. This woke Granddad. 'What's going on? Has something happened?'

Dad gripped my hand. 'Natalie, I have some terrible news,' he said. 'There's been an accident.'

I jumped to my feet in shock. 'An accident?'

'Yes, I'm afraid it's Tommy and the girls.'

My heartbeat was suddenly deafening. 'Tommy and the girls?' I mumbled.

'Yes, they have been involved in an accident. Natalie, they didn't make it.'

'That's not funny!' I shouted, refusing to believe him. I ran out of the bedroom and entered the front room, where a tearful Betty and two police officers greeted me. I stood glued to the floor, stunned. I didn't know what to say or do.

'Oh my god!' I eventually screamed, 'Oh my god, oh my god!' I was about to crumble to the floor when Mum caught me. 'Oh god, no!' I cried, 'please god, no no no!' I felt powerless. 'Tell me it's not true Mum,' I cried, 'please tell me it's not true!'

Everyone was in tears, even the police officers, as I continued to cry, hugging Mum with all my might. Then I fainted.

'Natalie, Natalie!' a voice called. Slowly I opened my eyes. I was being held by both Mum and Dad. They rested me gently on the couch as Betty took me into her arms. Granddad then handed me a large glass of undiluted Sunset Rum. Still in shock, I asked, 'What happened?'

The police officers explained that on the way home Tommy had swerved to avoid a drunk driver. As he did so, he had lost control of the car and it had catapulted over an embankment. He and my two lovely girls had been killed on impact.

I just went on crying, my entire body in agony. My life and my world had been turned upside down. 'Lord, why me?' I screamed, 'why me? What have I done to deserve this, why lord, why? I must go to them, Mum,' I sobbed, 'Tommy and the girls need me!' Barefoot, I ran towards the front door in a daze.

A short while later we all arrived at the local hospital. With trembling hands and knees and assisted by Betty and my devastated parents, we stood over the broken bodies of Tommy, Tina and Justina. I fell to the floor and screamed. I cried myself tearless. I felt so lost, so empty. They were my life, my world, what was I going to do without them? Could I live without them? Never! Never! Never!

I rose to my feet, and shaking them, shouted 'Wake up Tommy!' 'Wake up Tina, wake up Justina! Please wake up!'

Mum took hold of me. 'Natalie, Natalie, they're gone,' she cried.

'No Mum,' I screamed, 'look, they're asleep, they're just tired.'

'No my darling,' she cried, 'they're gone, gone forever.'

I ran out of the room, still with no shoes on. 'Natalie!' Mum called.

'I just need a few minutes on my own, Mum,' I managed to reply. Why had they left me, how could they leave me?

In a dreamlike state, I stepped on a bus that was about to depart, the last bus for the day. The driver and passengers all looked at me with deep sympathy, but no one said a word. They already knew what had happened. I could see tears on some of their faces. I sat down without paying, and no one spoke a word. The driver went straight on to Dickson village without stopping anywhere else.

When I got home, I went straight to the medicine cabinet. I opened it and looked at the three bottles of paracetamol inside. I grabbed them, and got some water. Then I swallowed the tablets as quickly as I could.

Still barefoot, not noticing the scratches and bloodstains I'd already picked up, I closed the front door and made my way slowly to top Dickson. I looked down at Dickson Village, beautiful, serene, lying there at the foot of the volcano. Here at the top of the hill I could look down at the place where Tommy and I had grown up. Our home.

I looked up at the now dormant volcano, whose violence had not so long before led to the evacuation of Dickson and all the surrounding villages. 'Life is a long, long road to travel,' I whispered softly. I started to head for home, but I staggered and fell to the ground, everything becoming faint. I could hear the voices of concerned villagers. 'Natalie, Natalie!' they were saying. But their voices grew fainter and fainter. In the distance I saw my Tommy, Justina in one hand, Tina in the other. I watched as they ran happily towards me.

'Tommy,' I called, 'Tommy my darling!' I closed my eyes and smiled in bliss. I was determined never to let Tommy and our precious little girls go again...

And then everything went blank.